CHRISTMAS MIRACLES

SIX SHORT STORIES OF GOD'S FAITHFULNESS IN ANY TIME, SPACE, OR REALM

CHRISTMAS MIRACLES

SIX SHORT STORIES OF GOD'S FAITHFULNESS IN ANY TIME, SPACE, OR REALM

JAKE TYSON   DANIEL PEYTON   LAUREN SMYTH

ALLEN STEADHAM   ERIC LANDFRIED   PARKER J. COLE

AMBASSADOR INTERNATIONAL
GREENVILLE, SOUTH CAROLINA & BELFAST, NORTHERN IRELAND

www.ambassador-international.com

Christmas Miracles

Paperback ISBN: 978-1-64960-611-2
eISBN: 978-1-64960-662-4

Cover design by Karen Slayne
Interior Typesetting by Dentelle Design
Edited by Katie Cruice Smith

AMBASSADOR INTERNATIONAL
Emerald House
411 University Ridge, Suite B14
Greenville, SC 29601
United States
www.ambassador-international.com

AMBASSADOR BOOKS
The Mount
2 Woodstock Link
Belfast, BT6 8DD
Northern Ireland, United Kingdom
www.ambassadormedia.co.uk

The colophon is a trademark of Ambassador, a Christian publishing company.

For unto us a child is born, unto us a son is given; and the government shall be on his shoulder: and his name shall be called Wonderful, Counsellor, The mighty God, The everlasting Father, The Prince of Peace.

-Isaiah 9:6 (King James Version)

Captain's Conundrum

Jake Tyson

CHAPTER 1

NOW

"The goat of Christmas past?" Fifteen-year-old Andrew Ashton frowned at the bleating baby goat standing on the tile kitchen floor. "Wasn't it supposed to be the ghost?"

A chorus of laughter pealed through the kitchen. Captain John Hudson crossed his arms over his chest and chuckled gently. Andrew was a kind, friendly soul. It was strange, having someone so young on a superhero team. John had become fiercely protective of Andrew since the boy's recruitment, but Andrew could take care of himself. Even missing the lower half of his left arm—or maybe because of it—Andrew was one of the toughest young men his age John had ever known. He certainly was not fragile.

DeAndre Knox, dark-skinned and twice Andrew's age, laughed and knelt next to the little white animal. He rubbed its head gently, causing the goat to let out another bleat. A paper sign was taped to the goat's side, with the words "Christmas Past" scrawled on it.

"You can't get a ghost at a petting zoo." DeAndre winked. "Besides, the Peacekeepers need a mascot, right? I saw this little guy and couldn't resist."

Andrew frowned. "I thought I was the mascot."

Beth Swift ruffled Andrew's shaggy brown hair. "You won't be a cute kid forever. One day, you'll grow up and be as ugly as DeAndre."

DeAndre scowled. "Uncalled for. I can take the goat back."

"No!" Beth hurried over and scooped up the animal in her arms. "It's too late. We've bonded."

"You've known him for less than five minutes," Andrew noted.

She nuzzled the goat's nose. "And I already love him more than any of you."

Andrew rolled his eyes and squeezed between DeAndre and Beth to get to the refrigerator. John stepped aside to let the team's final member, Maria Valdez, get a closer look at the goat. DeAndre had gotten the goat as a prank—after asking John's permission—and put it in Andrew's bed while the team was going through their morning training routine. Andrew had come into the kitchen, perplexed and frantic at finding the creature in his room and insisting, "It wasn't my fault!" Andrew had asked to keep a pet dog in the team's headquarters more than once, but John did not think his authorities would approve. Andrew had yielded to John's denial, but maybe he was afraid that John would blame him for the goat's presence.

"We're not really keeping the goat . . . are we?" Andrew asked.

John thought he detected a note of hope in Andrew's voice, masked by incredulity—if they could keep the goat, why couldn't he get a dog, after all? John chuckled gently but did not respond. He was the team leader, but he was not going to be the one to kill the jovial spirit in the kitchen—not this time, anyway. He would let them have their fun. They deserved it.

"U.S. Army regulations would suggest that keeping the goat would be frowned upon," Maria noted.

Beth quirked an eyebrow. "I hardly think we fall under typical U.S. Army standards. We wear colorful costumes into battle. Most of us fight with our fists. Face it—as far as the military is concerned, we don't exist, except as propaganda."

John grimaced. That was too true. It had been the president's idea to form a U.S.-hosted team of superheroes, especially with so many vigilante teams like the Vindicators running around. Some cities had their own teams legislated by the local government—like Juncture City's Justiciars—but the majority of superheroes were technically illegal. The president thought that a legitimized team would be good for national morale.

In all his years as a Green Beret, John never would have expected to be recruited for this kind of operation. He was a boots-on-the-ground kind of guy—a soldier, capable of giving or following orders, but just a soldier. He preferred anonymity. He never thought that he would be Captain Condor, the face of superheroes for the United States.

The United States government, he corrected himself. There was no doubt that when it came to superheroes as a whole, Gideon Turner—the Seraph—was the first face that came to most people's minds. He was the first, after all.

"A goat wouldn't do well in an environment like this, anyway," said DeAndre. "He should be somewhere more conducive to his needs—dietary and otherwise."

Andrew assembled a sandwich at impressive speed, putting together the components as quickly as someone with the use of both hands. As he worked, his expression drooped into a frown, but he did not slow at all. Maybe his ability to control time dilation for limited periods gave him a unique perspective on multitasking. There was no mistaking the change in demeanor, though. Whether he would admit it or not, Andrew was disappointed. John's heart ached for the kid.

"I don't see why he can't stay until Christmas, at least." John glanced at DeAndre and winked. "For mascot purposes, of course."

Andrew grinned. "Really?"

"Why not?" John chuckled. "Enjoy him while you can."

His sandwich forgotten, Andrew hurried to scoop the goat out of Beth's arms. Once again, John was reminded how young he actually was—and that no child should be in his position. It had been a point of contention between John and his superiors more than once and even between John and DeAndre, who had taken it upon himself to be Andrew's guardian on the team. John did not need convincing. Andrew should have been worrying about homework, girls, and saving money for a fast car, not about superhero training and fighting supervillains. DeAndre was even more outspoken about the fact than John was, but his superiors were adamant. Andrew being part of the team was good for their public image. John just hoped they didn't live to regret it. He had seen the consequences of this life firsthand. If Andrew suffered, John would never forgive himself.

Chapter 2

Deep breaths, deep breaths. John tightened his grip on his SCAR-H assault rifle and pressed his back against the cold wall of the cavern. Pitched in almost total darkness, he and his squad crept down the stone passageway single file, presenting as small a profile as possible. It all played out in front of him in shades of white and green, lit by his night vision goggles.

This cave was rumored to be the hideout of the terrorist known as Rasul al Nar—the Messenger of Fire. It was an appropriate name, John thought, if a bit on the nose. Rasul al Nar had done more damage to civilian targets in the last three months than some terrorists had in a decade. Getting a solid lead on al Nar's location meant they had to move in, whether the lead panned out or not.

"Stay tight." Phil Bosworth, the captain of John's unit, glanced over his shoulder. His voice was barely a whisper, but it came loud and clear through the earpiece inside John's helmet. "I've got movement ahead."

A hand patted John's shoulder twice. "Merry Christmas, John."

John glanced at his watch. Indeed, back home in the U.S., it was midnight—Christmas morning. *Sorry, Katy.* John wished he could be home with his fiancée to spend the holiday with her. But he knew his duty. Taking out Rasul al Nar would make people not just in the States but also here in Afghanistan far safer. If John could be part of that, he could not shirk it. Children in the surrounding villages could wake up and not worry about whether they might be blown up that day. In the grand scheme of things, that mattered most.

John glanced back over his shoulder at the man who had gotten his attention—John's best friend, Jovian Walker. John grinned and gave Jovian a thumbs-up. "Merry Christmas, buddy."

"Quiet." Bosworth raised his rifle. "Move in on my signal. Ready?"

John's palms broke out in sweat beneath his gloves. He adjusted his grip, brought the rifle to his shoulder, and peered down the sight. It was time to kill again. *Don't think about that. Think about who gets to live because of this.*

Bosworth's voice hardened. "Engage."

CHAPTER 3

NOW

A chill breeze swept across the avenue in downtown D.C. John's shoulders tensed beneath his brown jacket as the wind cut through him. Part of the advantage of John's powers was that he was more resistant to the elements than the average person, but he still was not a big fan of the cold. It reminded him too much of nights in the desert. His dark blue scarf fluttered, and he reached up to tuck it around his neck. Katy chuckled and leaned closer to him, bumping her shoulder against his arm. John smiled down at her.

Marrying her was unquestionably the best decision of his life. He questioned many other things on a regular basis. His military career, becoming a superhero, recruiting Andrew . . . How different would his life be now if not for those choices? What if he had become a firefighter, like he dreamed of as a child, or a motocross racer as his teenage self had envisioned? There were many paths John could have taken; but the one he had chosen led to Katy, so he always came back to a calm certainty that it was the right one. It was imperfect—painful at times—but she made it all worth it.

"How's the costume brigade today?" Katy asked.

John chuckled and wrapped his gloved hand around hers. Katy was never daunted by John's life as a superhero. In fact, she thought it was exciting. Maybe it was because she thought John was invincible now, since he had been too fragile as a Special Forces operative. He would never admit it; but sometimes as Captain Condor, he felt just as fragile as he ever had during his tours in Afghanistan.

"DeAndre got a goat." John shook his head, amused. "He put it in Andrew's room as a prank—he labeled it as the 'goat of Christmas past' for some reason—but Andrew fell instantly in love with the thing."

Katy laughed. "Oh, that's just mean, especially if he can't keep it."

"I told him he could keep it through Christmas. Where's the harm?"

"You big softie." Katy leaned her head on his shoulder as they walked. "You really care about that kid, don't you?"

John pressed his lips together. Yes, he cared about Andrew. He cared about all of them—DeAndre and Beth and Maria—but Andrew was special. He was one of the most real people John had ever met. There was nothing fake about him. He was enthusiastic, loyal, kind . . . He was just the kind of person who deserved to be a superhero. Someday, he would be a great one—maybe one of the best.

But he should not have been one at fifteen.

"I do." John bobbed his head. "I want the world for him."

"Are you sure you won't reconsider talking to the Pentagon about putting Andrew on inactive duty until he's seventeen?"

"I've tried. They say he's too valuable."

Katy gestured to the door of a shop they were passing. John turned and pulled the door open for her. Katy stepped inside; and John followed, relishing the warmth that closed around him as the door swung shut. He tugged his beanie off and tucked it into his jacket pocket. Katy reached up and gently combed John's brown hair to the side.

"Well, if the generals won't change their minds, you'll just have to keep an extra close eye on him." Katy grabbed a shopping basket. "Lucky for him, if anyone is up to the job, it's you."

Her confidence in him bolstered him. Katy had always been his biggest cheerleader, his rock when he had nothing to cling to. John was not a religious man, but he thanked God for her. Where would he be if he never had Katy? He imagined it would be a much darker place.

Chapter 4

It was a trap.

Rasul al Nar's men were lying in wait to ambush John's team as they moved into the cavern. A chaotic exchange of gunfire led to several of John's comrades falling, followed by the team being separated throughout the maze-like tunnels of the cave. The terrorists were hunting them now, and they had the home field advantage.

John looped his arm beneath Jovian's armpit, helping his friend stagger through the cave. Jovian had sustained a pretty serious injury during the initial exchange of fire. John panicked at the thought of something happening to his best friend. Jovian had to make it out of here. This life was hard enough with a loyal companion. Without Jovian, John wasn't sure if he could do it.

"Hang in there, buddy," John whispered.

Jovian coughed weakly. "It'll take . . . more than that to . . . take me out."

John swiveled his head, looking for a hiding place. There was a shallow recess in the cave wall to his right, deep enough to hide the two of them in its shadows. John eased Jovian into the opening and sat down next to him. Immediately, he pulled out his first aid kit and removed a syringe of painkiller and a roll of bandages.

"Intel." Jovian stifled a hacking cough. "What a . . . joke."

That cough didn't sound good. If Jovian had blood in his lungs, things were going to get bad fast. John had to get him out of the cave and to a medic. Unfortunately, who knew how many terrorists were between them and the exit? John would fight through them if he had to, but he couldn't do that and help Jovian walk at the same time. And he couldn't leave Jovian here, because he would be a sitting duck if the patrolling terrorists came upon him. Either way, their odds looked bad.

One problem at a time, he thought. John jammed the painkiller into Jovian and started bandaging the wound on his abdomen.

"You gotta go." Jovian put a hand on John's shoulder. "Gotta . . . get out. I'm history."

John shook his head. "Don't say that. I'm not leaving you here."

"Here . . . there . . . what does it matter?" Jovian patted his chest. "The part of me that matters will be somewhere better either way."

In moments like this, having religion like Jovian did must have been comforting. For him to believe that he would go to Heaven even if he died here . . . John wished he had that kind of peace. But right now, he was more concerned with getting Jovian back to his family. Telling them that Jovian was in Heaven would be a cold comfort. John wasn't sure how he would forgive himself if he had to tell them he had failed to bring Jovian home.

A sharp cough crackled over John's earpiece. "Anyone still alive? Report in?"

He recognized Bosworth's grizzly voice with a jolt. Somewhere in this warren, the captain was still hanging in there. Was he alone? John swung about to scan the tunnel for any sign of the terrorists before responding.

"Hudson here," he said. "I've got Walker, but he's in bad shape."

"I've got Thompson and Williams, but they're both dead." Bosworth coughed again. "I think I can draw their attention—give you time to fall back."

"Not without you, sir."

"Don't be an idiot. There must be a dozen of these guys between me and you. If I can draw them all to me, maybe you can get Walker out."

John swallowed. "Sir . . . the op."

"Op's blown. Rasul al Nar probably was never here. If he was, he's gone by now. But I can put a nice dent in his operations, at least. I saw a pallet of explosives in the central cavern."

John put the puzzle pieces together. Bosworth would cause a ruckus, draw the terrorists to the central cavern . . . and detonate the explosives. He would die taking out a chunk of al Nar's cell. Every fiber of John's being revolted at the thought of leaving Bosworth behind. This might be the only way to save Jovian, though.

"Okay, sir. I—"

Jovian's hand clamped over John's mouth. John's eyes widened. A beam of white light shone from around the corner. John fell back further into the alcove. That light could only have come from a patrolling terrorist—and if he shined it into this recess, John and Jovian were sitting ducks.

"God," Jovian whispered, "please avert their eyes."

CHAPTER 5

NOW

John and Katy spent most of their afternoon shopping for Christmas gifts. John was not good at picking out presents—he just saw items on a shelf, rarely associating them with the interests of his friends and loved ones—but Katy was great at it. She pointed out a movie collection that DeAndre would like, a practical organizational set for Maria, and a sports bottle with a lightning bolt on it for Beth.

Of course, John would have to pick Katy's gift out himself. Why was she so hard to shop for? She was his wife—he saw her every day and knew what every one of her interests were. Yet when he went to the store, he found himself staring with glazed eyes at the shelves, not a clue in the world what to buy her. It was like at that moment, she became a complete stranger to him. He always managed somehow, though.

That was a problem for another day. He couldn't shop for Katy while she was standing right beside him. He would have to take his own shopping trip before Christmas. He suspected she already had his gifts picked out—probably had for a long time. John was glad she never seemed to mind his ineptitude at these things.

"Okay, last person on the list is Andrew," Katy said. "Any idea what he might like?"

John shook his head, baffled. What did teenagers like these days? Video games, social media . . . He had no idea. Of course, the one thing Andrew really wanted was a dog, but that was beyond John's control. His higher-ups would never let him keep a pet on the base long-term, and Andrew already had a dog at home. John doubted Andrew's parents would want him to have another one, especially when his duties at the Peacekeepers' base kept him so busy, he hardly had time to take care of the one he already had.

John scanned the shelves of the thrift store they were currently browsing. His eyes fell on a glass case near the front of the store, which contained a variety of pocketknives and other small trinkets. One particular knife caught his eye—just over three inches long, the handle looked carved from wood. The blade was folded into the handle, but John could tell from the glimmer of the back edge that it was good quality. He asked the shopkeeper to see the knife and turned it over in his hands.

It reminded him of the pocketknife his grandfather had given him on his sixteenth birthday. That one had the name "Hudson" carved in the handle, and it remained one of John's most prized possessions. He ran his finger across the wood surface. It was fine craftsmanship. John suspected he could pay someone to carve Andrew's name into it without damaging the knife. He turned it over in his hands, considering. Was this the kind of gift Andrew would appreciate?

He was not sure, but something told him to get it.

"I'll take it." He handed the knife back to the shopkeeper. "It's perfect."

Katy blinked. "That was the fastest I've ever seen you pick out a present for anyone ever."

"I know." John chuckled. "Usually, I'm indecisive, completely at a loss; but this . . . I just know it's right."

She smiled. "I'm sure Andrew will love it."

"I hope so." John handed over his debit card, paid for the knife, and then took it in the small plastic bag the shopkeeper offered. "Come on. I need to find a woodworker to finish this gift. Then we can go home."

Katy took his hand. "Sounds like a plan to me."

Chapter 6

Two years ago

John shouldered his rifle and rested his finger on the trigger. Even if he shot the patrolling terrorist, though, the gunfire would echo through the tunnels, alerting others. Any hope John had of sneaking Jovian out while Bosworth caused a distraction would be lost. He found himself silently praying alongside Jovian, parroting his words.

Don't let them see us, don't let them see us . . .

John removed his night vision goggles. If the light shone on him directly, it would blind him, hindering his ability to fight back. Darkness enveloped him, pierced only by the gradually approaching beam of light. He stiffened, ready to go down shooting—

The light shone directly in his eyes. John prepared to meet a hail of gunfire . . . but the light swept right on past. Footsteps pattered against the cave floor. Slowly, they faded. John let out the breath he had been holding and sagged back against the wall, resting against Jovian.

"I don't understand," he breathed.

Jovian chuckled softly. "It's a Christmas miracle."

John frowned. Was that possible? Jovian had prayed for the terrorists to be blinded. Had God really done that? It was the only explanation John could think of. The light had shone right into that alcove. There had been no shadows to camouflage John and

Jovian—they were exposed. Somehow, the terrorist had just not seen them and carried on with his patrol. Divine intervention was the only answer. If there was any day of the year for it, John supposed it was Christmas.

Gunfire echoed through the caverns. John tensed again as the footsteps returned, but they hurried by the alcove in the opposite direction. *Bosworth.* It had to be the captain.

"Get out of here!" Bosworth growled over comms. "Hurry!"

John helped Jovian stand. Together, they limped back the way they came. They had to get to the exit fast. Bosworth was tough, but he was one man against an army. All it took was one lucky shot to bring him down. John hoped Bosworth could hold off the terrorists long enough for John and Jovian to get outside. He wished the captain didn't have to die, though.

All he could worry about now was Jovian. Bosworth was beyond help. John focused on putting one foot in front of the other and pressing on toward freedom.

Chapter 7

Now

The Peacekeepers' base was filled with state-of-the-art technology supplied by multiple government contractors. Sterling Enterprises, Garvin Technologies . . . the best of the best was brought together to ensure that the superhero team had everything they needed to handle whatever threats might be thrown their way. Part of that was preparing for those engagements before they happened. That meant training.

John stood in the control room that hung over the massive training complex—which Beth had aptly codenamed "the Course." From the control room, John could set the Course's automatic training programs, tailoring them to each member of the Peacekeepers to give them the toughest challenge.

With Christmas approaching, each of them would have a few days' leave. Though none of the Peacekeepers stayed on-base full time, it would be odd to have all of them gone. Before that happened, John wanted to get in a few more hours' training. There was no telling when an emergency might strike, and the extra preparation might come in handy.

Beth, dressed in her light blue and silver costume, darted through the Course, trailed by stun beams fired by guns mounted on the walls. She was known as Formula One—and John had seen few speedsters as fast as she was. Beth was one of their heaviest hitters because there were almost no threats that could keep up with her.

In an elevated section of the Course, Maria—aka Stillhouette—clung to the shadows as patrolling drones scanned for her. Maria's powers allowed her to camouflage herself in near-invisibility, gathering the shadows around her, which made her a useful stealth operative, but they were not as useful in active combat. To make up for that, Maria trained extensively in all manner of close-range fighting styles. She was good, but John wanted her to have a firm grasp on how useful her powers could be to the team. Today's objective for Maria was to stay out of the drones' sensors.

Andrew's yellow-clad form bounced up a series of platforms that seemed to be levitating. As Minuteman, Andrew had the ability to slow and manipulate time on a narrow scale. Right now, the platforms seemed to be floating only because Andrew had them in his time lock. They had actually fallen from the ceiling at normal speed. It was only Andrew's fine control that kept them in place long enough for him to climb them.

The only member of the team John did not see active was DeAndre, and that was because he was too small for anyone to perceive. DeAndre—Micron—could shrink down to the size of a paperclip. He was in his own little world right now. John's enhanced senses would have allowed him to see DeAndre and his black and blue costume clearly if he was down on the Course floor with the team; but from up here, he was not at the right angle.

John adjusted the flow of his white-trimmed blue cape over his red uniform. He was the last member of the Peacekeepers to join the training—it was time he got started. Activating the compressing walls on the south side of the Course, John dropped out of the control room. Most people would have considered John the most powerful member of the Peacekeepers. He was Captain Condor—he could fly, had super strength, was nearly invulnerable, and had senses so enhanced he could see and hear things happening miles away. Although he might be the most conventionally powerful, he did not underestimate the contributions each of his teammates made. Without them, he could not accomplish a fraction of the things he did. He needed them, just like they needed him.

The walls he had activated started closing inward. They moved slowly, but they weighed over three tons. Captain Condor flew directly in front of them, pressed his palms against the cold, reflective metal surface, and pushed. The gears contracting the walls groaned in protest. He clenched his jaw and pressed harder. Even if the walls broke past his hold, he was probably durable enough to survive their crushing force, but he was not inclined to find out. There was always the possibility that he was wrong.

It was important to push his limits, though. There was always the possibility that they would come up against a threat that Captain Condor could not punch his way past. He needed to be strong enough to protect his team.

His muscles strained against the pressure of the oncoming walls. Condor spread his feet and bent his legs, gathering his strength to push back. The walls moved inexorably forward, but he kept pushing back.

He would never stop pushing back. He couldn't. If Captain Condor let up, even for a moment, someone could die. And it was not just his team in danger or his loved ones. Innocent people who had done nothing to deserve disaster could die—everyday folks, just trying to claw out the best life they could manage. People like that did not deserve to have their lives disrupted by evil. That was why Captain Condor and the Peacekeepers were necessary to protect the people who could not protect themselves—people like Katy, who, in another life, could have had happiness, a family, a normal job.

People like Jovian . . .

Chapter 8

With every burst of gunfire that sounded behind him, John expected to take a bullet to the back. But the echoes were distant, coming from whatever corner Bosworth had sequestered himself in as he drew all the enemy fire toward him. John swallowed the lump forming in his throat. Bosworth was giving his life so John—and hopefully Jovian—could live. It was unfair. John wished he could go back and protect his commanding officer. But doing that would be pointless. John would just die with him, nullifying the sacrifice Bosworth was trying to make.

Jovian stumbled. "Can't . . . keep up . . . "

"We're almost there, buddy." John tightened his grip around Jovian's back and urged his friend on. "Come on. Don't you give up on me now."

Light shone from up ahead—but natural light. The first glimmers of sunlight cut far enough into the darkness of the cave to provide the barest illumination. John ripped off his night vision goggles and focused on heaving Jovian forward one step at a time. His friend was not so much limping as being dragged now. John could tell it was bad, but he had to keep going.

Something clattered behind John. He spun to find two terrorists hurrying up the tunnel behind him. He snapped up his rifle, fired two killing shots, and then resumed dragging Jovian the rest of the way outside. His feet met a soft patch of dirt. *Yes!* he thought.

He pulled Jovian to the side of the cave entrance, where he found a hiding place among some tangled brush. He eased Jovian down and turned, keeping his rifle shoulders.

"Captain?" John said into his mic with a shaky breath. "We're clear."

"It's been an honor, gentlemen," Bosworth grunted. "Godspeed."

Seconds later, the land around them rumbled as a deep *boom* sounded from within the cavern. John slumped down next to Jovian and looked over at his friend. Jovian was staring up at the morning sky, his eyes glassy.

"Thanks for trying, John."

"Trying?" John shook his head. "No, it's not over yet. Come on. Let's get you back to the Humvee. We can still—"

"No. I'm played out, man. You know it, too."

Tears brimmed in John's eyes. He did know it, but how could he admit defeat like this? He couldn't let Jovian die.

"Don't . . . forget the miracle, man." Jovian looked over at him and smiled. "God's good, man. Don't forget."

CHAPTER 9

NOW

"Cap? Captain!" A hand fell on his shoulder. "*John!*"

Condor snapped out of his reverie and realized that the walls he had been holding back were now dangerously close to closing in on him. DeAndre stood in the narrow gap with him, his dark brown eyes wide with concern behind his black and blue cowl.

"Turn off the machine!" Maria shouted.

A blur of light blue hinted at Beth's rapid motion as she disappeared up the stairs to the control room. John's muscles strained, and he pushed back just enough to keep the walls off him and DeAndre. A second later, the walls began to retract. John relaxed and slumped into a crouch. DeAndre knelt next to him and frowned.

"You okay, boss?"

John looked up. Andrew and Maria were standing right behind DeAndre, concern etched on their faces. John grimaced when he realized how deeply he had been lost in thought. Another few seconds and he might have found out whether his body was durable enough to handle the crushing walls. He pushed himself to his feet and cleared his throat. It was embarrassing enough to have his team witness something like that. To have to tell them it was because he had been distracted . . .

"I'm all right." He clasped DeAndre's shoulder. "Thanks for snapping me out of it."

"You're lucky Andrew noticed." DeAndre jerked a thumb at the teenager. "If he hadn't alerted the rest of us, we might not have realized what was going on until it was too late."

John smiled weakly at Andrew. "Thank you."

"Don't mention it." Andrew stepped forward. "Are you good?"

"Yes. I just . . . I was remembering something that happened to me a lifetime ago. I guess I lost focus."

Beth joined them. "You? Lose focus?"

"Are you sure you're all right, Cap?" Maria's expression was still incredulous. John could always depend on her to keep him accountable. "Do we need to talk?"

"No, I'm . . . I'm good." John raised his hands, palms out. "Really, it was just a fluke. I'm not losing it."

DeAndre cleared his throat. "All right, everyone. Let's give the man some space. I think we've had enough training for today, anyway. Let's break off."

John remained behind as the others trickled out of the Course. He scratched the back of his head and stared at the gleaming silver floor, confused by his own distraction. Maybe it was just being so close to Christmas—the anniversary of Jovian's death—that was throwing him. It would pass.

Don't forget the miracle. John wanted to remember. He really did. But every time he thought back to that day, all he remembered was losing his friend.

An alarm blared. John's head snapped up. *Mission alert.* Someone needed them. He leaped into the air and soared out of the Course to find the rest of the team.

By the time he reached the command center, everyone else was already inside. They were still wearing their uniforms, as well—there hadn't been time to change out of them before the alert sounded. As John hurried into the broad, technology-filled room, DeAndre looked over his shoulder.

"It's Null Point," he said. "He's on the warpath."

John grimaced. Null Point was a gravity-manipulating supervillain. Originally a scientist named Gerard Wilkinson, Null Point had watched his funding get cut by the U.S. government after his military projects got too ambitious and resulted in the deaths of several soldiers. He was one of the first supervillains the Peacekeepers had battled as a team; and until now, they'd believed he was still locked up.

"Where's he attacking?" John asked.

"Archbishop Carroll." Andrew's face was pale as he turned toward John. "That's my high school."

"A high school?" Beth scowled. "At least, we know he's not a supervillain with standards."

John was not surprised. The first day he had recruited Andrew to the Peacekeepers, a pair of thugs had attacked Andrew's school bus, attempting to abduct Andrew's friend Jill, the daughter of Senator Samuel Weston. John had never told Andrew, but he later learned that those thugs were employed by Null Point. Weston was the driving force behind shutting down Null Point's projects. If the supervillain was attacking the school now, it was a fair bet that he was after Jill again.

"Let's move, Peacekeepers." John withdrew his blue domino mask from his belt and brought it up to his eyes. "We've got to stop him before those kids are hurt."

DeAndre pulled on his cowl as he made for the door. "No worries, Cap. Hey, we've beat Null Point before. Maybe today will hold a little Christmas miracle for us."

John suppressed a grimace. As much as he wanted to believe in Christmas miracles, his history with them was not so great. But maybe DeAndre was right. Maybe today would be different.

Chapter 10

ONE YEAR AGO

It was two days until Christmas, and John was dreading the anniversary of Jovian's death with every passing day. John and Katy had gotten married six months ago, so his thoughts should have been occupied with planning for their first Christmas as husband and wife. Unfortunately, he kept reliving his friend's passing at the worst possible moments.

Since John's return from Afghanistan, he and Katy had been living in Raven City, Florida, where her family lived. John missed the cooler Virginia winters. Here in Florida, winter still felt like a cool summer afternoon. Part of John wished that his first American Christmas back from overseas was a more classic white Christmas. As long as he was with Katy, though, he was sure it would be a good one.

She was busy preparing her part of the Christmas Eve dinner they would share with her parents the following night, so John decided to get out of the house for a while. He went to his regular gym and found it nearly abandoned. After all, who worked out two days before Christmas? Everyone was either bracing themselves to indulge in overeating or rushing to the stores for last-minute shopping. John had the gym mostly to himself, and he could not say that he minded.

As he lifted weights, his mind drifted back to his last days with Jovian. His friend had always been upbeat, encouraging. He was the only one who made the living nightmare in Afghanistan bearable. If anyone deserved to come home intact, it was Jovian. What kind of injustice was it that he died—on a holiday celebrating the birth of his religion's Savior, no less—while John was the sole survivor of his team?

Don't forget the miracle. But why had God done the miracle, if Jovian was just going to die minutes later? Why had John been forced to see a glimmer of hope that God might let them survive, only to have it snatched away as Jovian died in a sandy patch of underbrush? Surely, God had not done the miracle for John. Why would He? John was not even sure he believed in God's existence, so why would God work a miracle to save someone like him?

If You really wanted me to believe in You, God, You should have saved Jovian, he thought.

John growled between gritted teeth as he pushed against the weights, his muscles burning and sweat beading on his forehead and neck. Then with a loud grunt, he slammed the weights back onto the rack. He stared at his reflection in the floor-to-ceiling mirror running the length of the gym's north wall. His dark hair was tousled, his beard thicker than usual. The last year had been tough.

But it had brought its share of good things, too. He had Katy, and she was the best thing that had ever happened to him. He had a new life—a safe life—away from the chaos of war. Things were not as bad as they seemed. He just missed his friend.

Across the gym, someone screamed. Frowning, John spun to look for the source. Years of training kicked in as he braced himself for confrontation. The few occupants rushed for the front door, including the employees. John caught the nearest man by his bicep and stopped him.

"What's going on?"

Wide-eyed, the man pointed to the back of the gym. "Bomb!"

CHAPTER 11

Now

The air high above D.C. was frigid, but Captain Condor's suit had been designed with a thermal underlay beneath the Kevlar-woven fabric. That, combined with his powers' natural resilience to the elements, meant that he was only slightly uncomfortable in temperatures that would have sent anyone else's teeth chattering. On the highway below, he spotted two motorcycles—black and blue for Stillhouette and Micron, with Minuteman riding in a yellow sidecar on Micron's bike—and Formula One's telltale blue streak.

"Remember, civilian safety is our priority," Condor said. "We have to stop Null Point, but there are kids down there whose lives are in danger. Keeping them out of harm's way comes first. Formula One, you're on crowd control. Keep those students and faculty out of the zone of engagement. Minuteman, slow any stray projectiles Null Point sends flying. Micron and Stillhouette, keep him occupied."

A chorus of "copy that" filled the comm line from his teammates. Last time the Peacekeepers had engaged Null Point, their victory had come when Andrew was able to slow Null Point enough for John to engage him before the supervillain could use his gravity manipulation powers. John doubted the same tactic would work twice, but he had tangled with Null Point enough to know that if he could just get his hands on the supervillain, the crisis would be over. Null Point's gravity powers were not strong enough to break Captain Condor's grip on him once the Captain had a hold.

"Man, don't supervillains take holiday breaks like everyone else?" Andrew complained.

If only, Captain Condor thought. He steeled himself and angled his flight to descend toward the school. He hoped they were not too late. Debris filled the air around the school, a whirlwind of detritus spinning at Null Point's whim. Some of the projectiles—clipboards, dodgeballs—were virtually harmless, but there were benches and playground equipment and even a few cars in the mix. Those could do real damage.

In the middle of it all hovered the white-armored supervillain himself, his face concealed by a visored helmet. A cape fluttered in the air behind him.

Condor's gaze hardened. "Peacekeepers, engage!"

He landed in a crouch and immediately spun to catch a Subaru SUV hurtling toward a pair of girls. The girls shrieked but then vanished in a trail of blue pseudo-motion as Formula One scooped them away. Captain Condor rested the SUV on the school lawn and spun to face Null Point—only to have to catch a ruler-sized Micron as he hurtled through the air.

Micron grimaced and leaped out of Captain Condor's grip, reverting to his original size. "Sorry, Cap. He caught me mid-leap."

Condor nodded. "We'll have to catch him by surprise."

Stillhouette was gathering a cloud of shadows around Null Point, attempting to blind him so he couldn't see what he was lifting. But as she did, a large tire slammed into her abdomen. She grunted and tumbled back. Condor hurried forward to catch her before she struck a tree. A light post slashed through the air toward them . . . and slowed to a crawl just before it would have impaled Stillhouette. Condor turned to find Minuteman standing nearby, the stump of his left arm extended as he held the post in slow motion. Captain Condor grabbed the post and rested it on the ground.

"Thanks," he said. "That was too—"

Someone shrieked. Condor turned to find Null Point ascending into the air, Jill Weston struggling in his gravitic clutches. Minuteman was already leaping toward her. His hand caught her ankle, and he rose after Null Point with her. A metal box struck Minuteman in the head. He slumped and released his grip on Jill but remained caught in Null Point's grasp. The supervillain soared away from the school, his hostages in tow.

No! Condor rocketed upward. He was not letting Null Point get away. He would not let Jill be taken, would not let Andrew get hurt. His eyes locked on Null Point, Captain Condor drew back a fist.

Something heavy slammed into him, and everything went dark.

Chapter 12

One year ago

Every survival instinct in John's body said to turn and flee from the gym as fast as he possibly could, along with the rest of the occupants. But his training reminded him, he didn't know how big the bomb's payload was. If it went off, it could well damage the buildings around it, not just the gym. Those buildings' occupants did not know about the bomb.

The bomb squad was probably already on the way. Katy would kill him for doing something stupid.

John turned and ran for the bomb.

He dropped into a crouch next to the device. Immediately, he could tell that it was not a normal bomb. Roughly the size of his torso and shaped like a pear, it was all dark gunmetal and lined with purple. *Who puts that much detail into a bomb?* There was a timer on the front.

00:45.

That did not give John much time to check its inner workings. Jaw tight, he found a panel beneath the timer and pried it open.

The bomb's inner workings were like nothing he had ever seen. Rather than a normal explosive payload, a vial of some bubbling greenish liquid was hooked to tubes and vents in the center of the bomb. Wires connected the central mechanism to the timer.

John's gut sank. He knew exactly what this was. For the last four months, gas bombs had been going off across the country, leaving in their wake new superhumans. The bomb was not lethal, then; but if it activated, the cloud of gas that would erupt was likely to cause everyone in the parking lot outside to become superhuman.

00:40.

John rushed for the front doors and locked them. Then, he did the same for the back exit. If he could not stop the bomb from detonating, at least he could contain the cloud. He hoisted the device, which was heavier than it looked, with effort and took it to the innermost part of the gym, the men's locker room.

00:22.

He placed the device in a shower, pulled the curtain shut—as if that would do much good—and turned to run. Odds were good that the gas cloud would find him no matter where in the gym he went; but maybe if he was far enough away, the gas would dissipate before it reached him. John really had no desire to become a superhuman.

As he neared the locker room exit, he heard sniffling from one of the toilet stalls. Eyes wide, he rushed back and knocked on the stall door.

"Is someone in there?"

A child's voice whined out. "Everyone ran. I'm scared."

No, no, no. How long was left on the timer? Ten seconds? Less? John kicked in the stall and scooped up the child—a boy no older than ten, probably at the gym with a parent—before turning again to flee the locker room. He pushed the door open . . .

Boom.

CHAPTER 13

NOW

Captain Condor swam back to consciousness, the gray skies and an assortment of objects above him blurry and indistinct in his jarred vision. Something rested on his chest. He blinked twice. Slowly, everything came into view. Micron and Stillhouette knelt next to him. They were beneath the large oak tree in the schoolyard. Condor jerked upright.

"Andrew!"

"Easy, Cap." DeAndre helped John lean against the tree. "You got hit with a school bus. I'm not kidding. Null Point literally threw a bus at you."

John grimaced. So, that was the impact. It was a testament to his powers that he was not dead right now. Or maybe, DeAndre would have said, it was a Christmas miracle. John did not care either way. Right now, all that mattered was finding Andrew. He pushed himself to his feet and groaned as pain shot through the left side of his body.

Maria whistled. "I can't believe you're standing. We need to get you back to base and have a medic check you over."

"Not until Andrew and Jill are safe." John grimaced. "Why are you two standing around? We should be following them."

"Beth's hot on Null Point's heels, following him from the ground," DeAndre said. "She's got her transmitter live. Your enhanced hearing should be able to pick it up even miles away."

"How long was I out?"

"Only a couple minutes." Maria shook her head, sending her short bob of hair waving in the air. "You're one tough customer, John. And I know you want to get the kid back; but I must reiterate, standard protocol after taking a blow like the one you did would be to—"

"I'm not stopping." John clenched his fists. "Not until Andrew's safe. You two stay here and help the authorities with cleanup. Look pretty for the cameras. Reassure the media that we're on the case and Senator Weston's daughter will be returned safely."

DeAndre's brow furrowed in concern. "John . . . "

He didn't wait to hear their arguments. Captain Condor blasted into the air and listened for Formula One's transmitter signal. Even among the chaotic noises of traffic, he picked it up in seconds. She was heading out of D.C. toward a densely wooded area. Ignoring the pain in his entire left side, Condor rocketed after her—and hopefully, her targets.

He ascended until he was nearly in the clouds, far enough above the city that the white noise faded to a mild irritation. Formula One's signal, though, came in loud and clear. Captain Condor narrowed his eyes and scanned the land below. He spotted Formula One darting down a highway lined with snow-capped trees. Between them, Null Point's white armored form flew above the woods, still trailing Andrew and Jill's flailing forms. Andrew was conscious again, at least. He might be able to help Condor take Null Point down and get Jill to safety.

"I've got them, F-One," Condor said. "Keep pace and be ready to recover Minuteman and Jill when they come down."

"Copy."

Best way to do this is fast. If Null Point saw Condor coming, he would simply alter the gravity in the air surrounding Condor and render his flight capabilities useless. The captain extended both arms in front of him, hands balled into fists, and shot toward Null Point at speeds that would have impressed Formula One.

He struck Null Point like a bullet. The supervillain grunted as Condor collided with him. He spun and swung a wild punch, but Condor blocked it with a forearm and drove his forehead into Null Point's helmet. The dark visor shattered, and shards of the white helmet tumbled to the woods below. Null Point wiped blood from his nose and scowled.

Condor looked down. There was no sign of Andrew or Jill. Fear gripped his heart, and he hoped Andrew had been able to use his time powers to slow their fall.

"F-One, do you have them?" he asked.

"I lost sight behind the trees when they fell!" she replied. "I'll have to scan the forest on foot, but it'll be slow going."

Condor dodged another punch. "Do it!"

He grabbed Null Point's armor and pulled himself close. As long as he was holding on to the supervillain, Null Point's gravity powers were useless. He couldn't affect Condor without also affecting himself. That gave Captain Condor an advantage. He was much stronger—all he had to do was render Null Point unconscious, and this would all be over. Null Point snarled at him, his mane of graying hair flailing wildly in the wind, and jammed his fist into Condor's gut.

The blow hardly registered.

Condor shook his head, smirked, and brought his knee up into Null Point's jaw. The supervillain's eyes rolled back into his head. Before he could fall from the sky, Condor scooped him up and draped him over his shoulder.

"Null Point's down," he said. "See anything, Formula One?"

"Negative, Cap." Formula One swallowed. "I can't find them."

CHAPTER 14

ONE YEAR AGO

The world came back in a gradual blur before John's eyes. His ears rang, muffling all other sounds around him. Grimacing, he shifted and tried to get his bearings. Years of military training kicked in, his body instantly going into fight mode. His fists clenched; and he swung over to lie on his stomach, so he could press his knees into the ground and rise quickly.

A hand fell on his shoulder. John spun and lashed out with a fist but stopped his hand a millimeter short when he found himself looking in the face of a masked firefighter, who was almost a head shorter than John but solidly built. Despite the fear in his eyes, the firefighter didn't flinch.

"Are you all right, sir?"

John frowned and looked around. He was still in the gym. How long had he been out? Other law enforcement agents and first responders swarmed the building. There was no sign of the gas the bomb had released, so John must have been unconscious at least long enough for it to dissipate.

He nodded. "I'm all right. The kid?"

"Already taken outside." The fireman glanced at the floor. "Sir, do you think you could touch the ground for me?"

Touch the—? John dropped his gaze and realized his feet were hovering over six inches off the speckled tile floor. The firefighter was not shorter than John—he was *below* him. Eyes wide, John cast about. What did he do? How did he get down? What if he never figured out how to touch the ground again? His heart pounded and leaped into his throat.

"Easy, sir." The firefighter held out his hands, palms up. "You're okay. This has been happening to a lot of folks lately, but they always get it under control. You can do this. Focus."

John took a shaky breath. *Focus.* He could do this. He had fine-tuned his control over his body during his time as a Green Beret. Slowly, John imagined himself lowering to the ground . . . and his body followed the thought. John's shoes scraped against the tile. With a sigh, he rested his hand against the firefighter's shoulder.

"Thank you."

The responder nodded. "No problem. You were real brave, doing what you did. Stupid, but brave. Come on. Let's get you outside."

John chuckled at the firefighter's honesty. He was right: it had been stupid. But John had not been thinking about anything other than protecting as many people as he could. Jovian would have chewed him out to no end. Katy was going to have a fit when she—

"Johnny!"

As he exited the gym, she rushed to him and wrapped her arms around his neck, burying her head in his shoulder. John embraced her in return. After a moment, she looked up at him with a rueful smile, tears in her eyes, and shook her head.

"You just have to be the hero, don't you?"

John chuckled. "Sorry if I scared you."

She slapped his chest. "You sure did. Don't ever do that again!"

"Hopefully, it'll never come up again."

John suddenly realized that the air was actually chilly. Despite his short sleeves, it didn't register at first; but Katy's skin was covered in goosebumps. John frowned and looked up. The sky was completely overcast, unlike the clear afternoon when he had walked into the gym; and it had to be twenty or thirty degrees colder.

"What's going on?" he asked.

Katy stepped aside and gestured behind her. The EMTs had the little boy John had saved on a stretcher, but the boy was conscious. Wide-eyed, he was staring at the sky. Snowflakes rose from the palms of his hands. As if in response to the phenomenon, more snowflakes dropped from the clouds. John exhaled and saw his breath form in the air before him. *The boy got weather-controlling powers.*

John pursed his lips. Just a few moments ago, he had been wistful for the cooler winters of Virginia. Now, it was snowing in Florida?

Jovian would have called it a miracle. John wasn't so sure. But right now, he was just grateful to be alive. That was a miracle enough by itself. As for his powers, time would tell if those were a miracle as well or if they were a curse.

Chapter 15

Now

Did I get them killed?

John flew back and forth over the woods, scanning for any sign of Andrew or Jill. In the midst of his fight with Null Point, he had not seen where the kids had fallen. When Beth lost sight of them, there was no telling how fast they had been falling or how deep into the woods they might have been. What if John's haste to attack Null Point before the villain saw him had doomed an innocent girl to death?

What if it had doomed Andrew?

He refused to give those thoughts credence. Jill and Andrew were alive out there somewhere. They had to be. *If there's a God, they have to be alive.* John had taken Null Point back to DeAndre and Maria to arrest him and then quickly rejoined Beth in the woods. He had been searching since. It had been hours, and the temperature was dropping as the sun fell to meet the horizon.

John did not care how cold it got. He could stand it. He would send Beth back to base if he had to, but he was not leaving until he found those kids. There was no chance of that. Two Christmases ago, he had lost Jovian, despite seeing a miracle. Last Christmas, he had saved a child, resulting in what he thought of as another miracle. He was determined that tonight would be more like last Christmas than the one before.

If he could just have one more miracle . . .

He should have been able to see the bright yellow of Andrew's costume from far away; but the foliage was so thick, even his enhanced vision only saw a blur of browns, grays, and whites. If Andrew was down there, he had to be hidden beneath the branches of a tree big enough to block John's field of vision.

"Anything, Cap?" DeAndre asked over comms.

"Nothing." John clenched his jaw. "They're here somewhere. I know it."

"You'll find them. If anyone can . . . "

I hope you're right. "As soon as Null Point's locked up, get back to base and gather whatever equipment you think will be useful. Heat sensors, motion detectors—anything. I'm not leaving them out there overnight. They'll freeze."

"Andrew's suit has thermal padding." DeAndre's voice softened. "That won't do much for Jill, though."

"They're both coming home, DeAndre."

John deactivated the communication line for the moment, setting it to alert him with a ping if any of the others tried to contact him. Andrew's earbud must have been knocked out or damaged if he had not tried to call yet—either that or Andrew himself was incapable of making the call. Unconscious?

Dead?

No. He wouldn't consider it.

God, I told You that I would've believed if You had saved Jovian. Here's another chance to make me believe.

Minute after endless minute passed. With every second, the sun dropped closer to the horizon, and the temperature fell. Even John was beginning to feel the effects of the cold now, even if he was able to endure it. He had to find them soon.

A shape moved in a clearing below. His heart pounding, John circled around and peered down into the clearing, using his amplified vision to see up close what would have been tiny to a normal human eye. A man stood in the clearing below, waving up at him with one arm and gesturing into the woods with the other. *Did he find them?* The man was clad in a heavy coat and hat, but his dark skin was just visible and—

Impossible.

It was Jovian.

How could it be? He had to be seeing things, right? He had seen his friend die, carried his body back to base, attended the funeral. This had to be a dream. But whether he was hallucinating or the man in the clearing just looked like John's old friend, he had to check. He would take any chance that might lead him back to Andrew. John dropped toward the clearing like a rocket. He landed in a crouch. His head came up, and he looked around.

There was no one in the clearing.

John narrowed his eyes and scanned the sparse woods around the clearing. As fast as he had landed, there was no time for not-Jovian to have disappeared. Yet there was no sign of the man now—not even cracked twigs or footprints in the snow to give him away. *What?*

John stood from his crouch, shook his head, and turned to launch himself back into the sky—until he caught a glimpse of yellow behind the trees.

Andrew?

John rushed toward the color. "Minuteman? Minuteman!"

A petite form leapt into view. It was Jill! "Over here!" she shouted. "Over here! He's hurt!"

John hurried to Jill's side. Andrew was sitting on the ground with his back to the tree, his head hanging limply against his chest. John knelt and checked on the young man. His vitals were steady, and he did not have any serious cuts or bruises.

"What happened?" John asked.

"He slowed us down, so we didn't get hurt when we hit the ground," Jill said. "But I think it wore him out. He passed out as we were walking through the woods, and he's been out since. I know who he is. His hair, the missing arm . . . He's my best friend, Andrew. You've got to help him! He saved me. If he hadn't been there, who knows what that maniac would've done to me? I need him to be okay."

"He will be." John scooped Andrew into his arms. "Climb onto my back. I'll carry you to the road, and then Formula One can run you back to town."

"O-okay."

Jill leaped up onto John's back and wrapped her arms around his neck. John stepped out into the clearing, looked up into the sky . . . and paused before he took off.

Thanks for sending Jovian, God.

Chapter 16

ONE YEAR AGO

Christmas Day led to the uncomfortable discovery that John's powers were not limited to flight. He heard every drip of liquid from the coffeemaker as Katy prepared his morning brew. He saw every follicle of hair on his face as he looked into the mirror to trim his beard.

When he went ax-throwing with Katy's brothers, he discovered that he was strong enough to hurl the entire ax through the target board and the wall behind it.

Despite his discomfort and the difficulty adjusting to his new abilities, John thought they could be useful someday. He seemed like a freak right now, sure; but with time and training, he might just make something of himself. Superheroes were all over the news lately—the Seraph, Spright, Aria, and the rest. John didn't know if he was ready to put on a colorful costume, but it would be unfair to keep powers this amazing to himself.

Jovian would have encouraged him to use them.

Just before New Year's Eve, John and Katy received a visitor. A man in a dark uniform stood on their front porch. Katy, clearly uncomfortable, let the man in. John stepped forward to shake the hand of the short, muscular man with slate gray hair.

"John Hudson? My name's Marcus Kane. I'm with the government, and I'm here to talk to you about your powers. I know you're served your country before, son, and we may have a way for you to do it again . . . "

CHAPTER 17

NOW

The relief in the atmosphere of the Peacekeepers' base was palpable. Andrew recovered quickly once he was wrapped in warm blankets and given plenty of fluids. DeAndre suspected that the exertion of his powers on such a scale had put Andrew into a kind of coma to recover his strength and that he should be totally fine in a few days. Andrew, for his part, was relieved that Jill was back home safe and did not even seem to care that she knew his secret identity.

The next night, the Peacekeepers sat on couches and armchairs in the base's lounge area as they exchanged gifts. Andrew had his goat—Christmas Past, or whatever he had decided to name it—on his lap, and the little creature was bleating gleefully. Beth was mooning over it. It was going to be hard to give that goat back to the petting zoo—but that was the best place for it, John knew. The others did, too.

John gathered his presents into a neat pile on the floor next to his armchair, safely out of the way. He had been given a few thermal sweatshirts, a compass, and a legitimate, licensed Captain Condor wristwatch, courtesy of Beth. John looked down at the watch face and shook his head. He did not even recognize his own cartoon visage on the body of the hulking red-clad superhero emblazoned on the watch.

"Is that everything?" Maria asked.

John picked up the wrapped box on the other side of his chair. "One last thing. This one's for Andrew."

The boy's eyebrows perked up. John crossed the room and handed him the box. Beth took Christmas Past from Andrew, allowing the boy the freedom to tear into the present. He withdrew the pocketknife—complete with his name carved into the handle—and stared at it with eyes as wide as saucers.

"This is awesome," he said. "Thanks, Cap!"

John reached over and ruffled his hair. "Anytime, kiddo. Anytime."

Chapter 18

ONE YEAR AGO

"So, do you think you'll take him up on it?" Katy asked.

John pressed his lips together and pondered the question as Katy slid under the covers of their bed. Marcus Kane's offer was a big deal— the opportunity to lead a government-fronted team of superheroes, be the face of "amplified people" and the official leading superhero of the United States. Apparently, someone at the Pentagon thought John was the right man for the job because of his past military service.

Taking the job would mean moving back to D.C., working with image consultants and marketers and all other kinds of propagandists; but it would also mean being able to do something good with his powers without becoming a vigilante. Something about the idea was attractive to John.

"Would you really be okay with moving away from your family?" he asked.

Katy tilted her head. "I'd miss them. And I definitely prefer Florida to Virginia, but . . . I saw the look on your face when Kane offered the position. You want to be a hero. That was the happiest I've seen you since before Jovian died."

"No, baby." John reached over and touched her face. "The happiest I've been since then was the day I married you."

"Okay, maybe happy was the wrong word." Kate considered in silence for a moment. "Most at peace, then."

John swallowed, pondering the words. He had to admit, she was right. Ever since he had saved that boy in the gym, his life had suddenly felt different—like he had a purpose again. Jovian's death had robbed him of something . . . Maybe it was peace. Could he really find peace in his own life again by becoming a superhero?

"You don't have to decide tonight," Katy noted.

"No . . ."

"But you already know what you're going to do."

Tears welling in his eyes, John nodded. "I think I do."

CHAPTER 19

NOW

Christmas with Katy in D.C. was entirely different from last year's in Raven City. John still woke up to the smell and sound of coffee brewing, though; and he was more than happy to down the contents of the mug she handed him. After the stress of nearly losing Andrew and the days of relief after, John needed downtime.

He also needed to think. There was no denying that someone had been in that clearing, pointing him to where to find Andrew and Jill. Likewise, there was no denying that the man had looked just like Jovian. There had been no footprints to prove anyone was there, but John knew what he had seen. He had not told anyone, not even Katy. But he knew.

And it had happened just after John's prayer.

He had a lot of thinking to do. It was too big a coincidence, in his mind, for him to reject the idea of God any longer. Clearly, there was a Deity out there Who could hear—and listened to—prayers. John needed to do some research. Jovian was not his only Christian friend. John's own brother was a pastor in Philadelphia. He would call him to get the answers he needed. Once he had gathered information, he could make a decision. For now, though, he decided it was enough to know God existed and to determine that he would learn more about Him.

Katy settled on the couch with John, half-sitting on his lap, her legs stretched out over the unused cushions. She wrapped her arms around John's neck, brought herself in close, and kissed him firmly on the lips. John allowed himself to get lost in her for a moment, enjoying the softness and the sweet taste of her lips. Finally, she pulled back, smiling broadly at him, and put a present in his hands.

"Merry Christmas," she said.

John opened the present, and his heart stopped. A positive pregnancy test rested on top of a pile of tissue paper inside the box. Eyes wide, he looked up at Katy.

"Really?"

She nodded. "We're having a baby."

Laughing, John hugged her exuberantly—careful not to break her with his strength—and leaped into the air. He soared around the confines of the living room with her in his arms; and then they floated together, hovering between the floor and the ceiling. His life was not perfect. He had endured his share of losses. and he still had a lot of decisions to make. Right now, though, he had one more miracle to celebrate.

"One little miracle of our own," he said.

Clockwork Magi

Dan Peyton

Chapter 1

Street cars trundled over the brick streets with steam spurting out small pipes on top and out the back. Josh rushed across the busy intersection, racing between walking people, soldiers, and ten cars. He came to a quick stop when a triple-decker bus drove right in front of him. He coughed hard at the billowing steam that belched out the back.

"Hey! Kid!" A soldier ran toward him.

"Oh, man. Not today." Josh hurried through the cloud of steam and dodged three cars to get to a throng of moving citizens.

"Kid!" the soldier yelled.

Pressing the satchel of rolled up parchments against him, Joshua lowered himself as best he could. He rushed between people, stepping on toes and bumping into baskets and purses. When two other soldiers looked for him, he found two ladies in enormous dresses admiring shoes in a shop window. He got between them and the window, pretending to be looking as well. Their large dresses hid him from the soldiers.

"Idiots," he muttered and exited the curtains of cloth that saved him.

As he turned another corner, two hands grabbed his arm. "Stop right there."

Josh gulped and looked up at the strict face of the first soldier to call out his name. "Oh, hello. I didn't see you."

"Sure, you didn't. Show me what's in the satchel," he demanded.

Joshua cleared his throat and opened it, not offering to take out the contents. "Uh, it's just some parchment I'm delivering."

"You make deliveries to the mages, and we want to know what you have this time."

"The mages are not your enemy."

"The mages don't like the empire, and they work to help our enemies. We just can't prove it. Now, show me those parchments!" He reached inside and pulled out a scroll.

"Don't damage it." Josh called out.

The man unrolled the parchment with a deep frown. "A star chart? What sort of battle plan is this?"

"Like I should know. I'm just the delivery boy."

"Sure, you are; and you only deliver to the mages. Now, tell me what kind of secret the mages are keeping from the emperor." The soldier continued to examine the parchment.

"Why don't you ask them yourself?" Josh said.

The soldier rolled up the parchment and shoved it into the satchel, bending it. "Funny, real funny. How would you like me to take you in?"

A nice-looking man in a suit and top hat adorned with goggles stepped up. "What seems to be the problem?"

The soldier turned, and the color in his face drained. "Oh, it's you, Master Mel. I was just questioning this boy with suspicious materials."

Mel smiled. "Oh, looks like the parchments that were being brought to my laboratory. Surely, you aren't worried about them."

"I'm going to take him in for questioning."

Mel responded with as much composure as if he were simply telling the man the time of day. "And just what would your superiors have to say about apprehending a child who is carrying nothing but star charts? I'm sure they would be so pleased with you wasting their time."

A million thoughts flashed in the soldiers' eyes, each one making him angrier. Finally, after mulling over options that were sure to fail, he shoved the boy toward Mel. "Fine, take him. But don't think we aren't watching you, Mage."

Josh waited while the soldier left. "He almost had me."

"Don't worry, he had no chance of taking you in. But let's not give him time to figure out another plan to bother us."

Josh followed Mel through the city, leaving its boundaries to find open fields with farmers hard at work. Soon, they came to the edge of the coast. An island sat off shore with a tremendous castle-like structure. It had pipes and gears running all over it, with three smoke stacks producing three different colors of steam. A bridge connected to the island but was lifted high into the air. Mel pulled out an elaborate key that was larger than his hand. He plugged it into a hidden location on the ground. Gears and cogs moved on the bridge, and it lowered. As it did, a pillar rose from the water to meet it so that it had support between the land and the island. Finally, it was down, and they could walk across.

Josh remained marveled as he walked across the bridge and up to the building. He paused and held up the satchel. "Uh, here you go."

Mel laughed. "Thank you, but I think you should come in."

"In there? I've never been inside. I've never crossed the bridge. You always come to me to get my deliveries."

Mel used the same key to open the front door. As it unlocked, the bridge returned to an upright position. "It seems the empires' eyes have fallen on you, and that means you're at substantial risk. I think you should come in and be safe in here for now. However, if you wish, you can go home to your family."

"I don't have a family. Mom and Dad are both gone."

"Such a pity."

"I've always wanted to see the inside of this place," Josh admitted.

"Then, do come in."

CHAPTER 2

JOSH FOLLOWED THE MAGE INSIDE his laboratory. The legends, fables, myths, and horror stories of these places rolled around his head. However, the kindness and gentleness of the man seemed to push any concern to the back of his mind.

Gears and cogs lined the walls, all turning and moving to work the place in ways Josh couldn't even fathom. Steam spewed and spurted at random within the highest places. The floor was made of glass, giving a clear view of all the pipes that ran beneath their feet. Intricate, delicately designed metal work graced corners and doors, giving beauty among the industrial elements.

"This place is amazing," Josh whispered.

Mel laughed. "You haven't seen the best part of it. Come on; keep up."

Josh hurried behind Mel. Pausing at the threshold of a door, he beheld a magnificent library that was all around him. The central room of this place was a giant cylinder that rose three stories high and six stories below where they stopped walking, making ten full levels. The walls were filled with books, scrolls, crystals, mirrors, and other items that were designed to hold information. The railing that held the walkways was gilded metalwork with leaf and flower patterns all along every inch.

"The library—the heart and soul of a mage's work," explained Mel. "Come, we need to get to the base floor."

"How?"

Mel stepped up to the railing and opened a gate. A small hot-air balloon rose and met them. It carried a gondola with four chairs on it and a control station in the middle. Mel helped Josh into it and then took a seat. He used the controls and navigated them down the many floors to the bottom.

The lowest floor had a large table in the middle, several smaller tables around the perimeter, and a desk. Everything was covered in books and paper, among many other small objects. A pedestal held a glass viewing screen connected to many cables.

"What is this place? Do you do your magic here?" Josh asked.

Mel smiled. "Mages don't do magic; that's just a silly belief among the people. We have a much greater power than magic—knowledge."

"Knowledge?"

"Yes. Mages have been around for a long time. We study everything and record what we learn in any form of recordkeeping that we can. We transcribe and trade our manuscripts with each other. We also collect anything written by other scribes. I have written works among my collection that date back centuries."

"What good is keeping a bunch of books and scrolls?"

Mel gestured around him. "Weapons don't win wars; knowledge does. Weapons don't bring peace; knowledge does. Knowledge is wisdom; wisdom is the greatest asset a human being can have. We mages have been advising kings and emperors for centuries, passing our wisdom to them. Now, if they refuse to heed our knowledge, then it's on them when they make stupid mistakes."

"Have you tried to tell the emperor to stop hurting people?" asked Josh.

"The empire we live in today is not governed by a single person but by a senate of people who are power-hungry. One thing the mages have learned is that when power lust enters the mind, wisdom is quickly pushed aside and scorned. I could no more sway the senate to stop persecuting people than I could convince the sun to not rise." He brushed a pile of papers off the large table. "Now, let's look at those charts."

Josh held up his satchel and pulled out scroll after scroll. Mel took them and unrolled each, placing stones on the corners to keep them open. "What do you need all these star charts for?" asked Josh.

Mel tapped his chin as he looked at them. "I need to study the stars to see their movements."

"Why?"

Mel smiled. "I love to hear that word. You want to learn, and I would love to teach. There's something unusual in the stars recently—a new star that seems out of place. I could be wrong, and it might have shown up at another time; so I'm going to study these charts that were created a long time ago. If I can find that star, then I will know more about why it's here today. Right now, I need a book . . . Let me see. *Algar's Comprehensive Guide to Star Movement* should help."

"What?"

Mel walked over to the wall and opened a panel filled with buttons. "Let's see. That would be in section eight. Algar . . . Algar . . . " He consulted a catalog of numbers. "Ah, number 5578." As he said each number, he punched a different button.

Creaking gears and spurts of steam echoed around them as a mechanical arm appeared out of the ceiling high above them. It rotated around and then reached into a shelf five floors up. Delicately pulling out a single book, it lowered back down and presented it to him.

"Ah, good, I put it back in the right place. It can be so hard when I forget to put them back. I haven't had an apprentice to help for years." He opened the book and flipped through the pages.

Josh hopped up. "Can I help?"

Mel put the book down and frowned at the chart. "It seems the book references two comets, and there's a meteor shower next month. This is the wrong chapter. Lemme see." He flipped more pages.

"Uh, Master Mel? Can I help?"

Mel looked at him. "What . . . oh, you want to help?"

"I could help around here. You know, be an apprentice."

Mel gave him a long stare and then said, "I could use a little help. Why don't you put those books away?" He gestured toward a table full of books. "Just follow the numbers. Use the lift; the center button will take you to any floor. The first number in the book's listing is the floor; the other numbers denote which place on the shelf to put them. You can read numbers?"

"Sure." Josh grabbed the stack of books and jumped onto the lift. He looked at the first and found it was 74075. Punching the number "7" on the little panel in the middle of the controls, the balloon lifted him up through the heart of the library.

CHAPTER 3

MEL ASCENDED THE LIBRARY ON the balloon lift. Level after level passed by until he had reached the summit of this mountain of knowledge. He climbed a set of metal stairs that led to the roof, where there were several chairs, cushions, and a low table. The view from this far up was glorious, especially at this late hour when the sky was full of stars and the moon reflected on the waters of the sea.

Laying in a lounge chair, snoring, was Josh. He had a book beside him, which was still open to the last place he had been reading.

"Josh. Josh." Mel kindly nudged him awake.

Josh's eyes trembled open. He suddenly recalled where he was. "Oh, sorry. I, uh, just . . . I got all the books put away . . . Then I found this place, and I found a book that looked interesting. And I was just looking at it and . . ."

"Don't worry. I love to see people learning, especially the youth." Mel took a seat next to him. "You did a fine job. Do you really want to be a part of this—to learn about the library and how to be a mage?"

"Yes, sir. I would love that."

"Good. Now, you know you'll have to live here. It'll be your new home. You're from the Cantha province, a good distance from here."

"How'd you know?" Josh sat up on the edge of the seat.

"I've learned a lot about you over the last few months. I needed a courier I could trust who would get my orders brought to me without being caught by the Imperials. You don't have any ambition to be part of the legion; you don't like the Imperials; and you have a good work ethic. So, I requested you each time I had an incoming order."

"That's why Mr. Trilon was always giving me these jobs. I thought I was just lucky. Most kids don't get regular work."

Mel smiled. "Most kids want to become soldiers and are distracted by all the Imperials walking around. You don't like them too much, do you?"

Josh snarled. "Imperials killed my parents. They accused Dad of being a spy and Mom of being a conspirator. My parents were just cheesemakers from Cantha. They never worked against the empire. But they got no trial, no judge—just execution. I don't like the empire."

"Sorry to hear that about your parents. I don't care for this empire, as well. Those who govern it are paranoid and disregard life far too often. Who they can't subjugate, they attack and distrust."

"Yeah," Josh agreed, "but they'll get theirs one day. My mother used to tell me stories of a great prophecy."

"What prophecy?"

"One day, a great military leader will come. He will return the temple to the children of God, and the kingdom of His people will be made whole again. He will overthrow evil tyrants and defeat the empire."

"You speak of the Messiah prophecies."

"Yes. My family was not native to Cantha. Mom and Dad were from the Judine province."

"Ah, now I understand why the empire distrusted them. No province has had more rumblings of revolt or rebellion than the Judine province. However, most of those rumors are untrue."

"Mom and Dad were not rebels or—" Mel held up his hands. "Don't yell at me. I trust you. The empire is foremost paranoid. Believe me, we mages have faced their paranoia for years."

"Sorry."

"It's okay. Now, I'll show you to your room, and you can get some sleep. We have a big day tomorrow."

"What's happening?"

"Just wait and see. Come on, first we'll have something to eat; and then it's bedtime."

CHAPTER 4

IT SEEMED JOSH HAD ONLY just settled down enough to fall asleep when a loud rumbling startled him awake. He hurriedly dressed and rushed down the hall toward the nearest window. With a giddy gasp, he beheld a medium-sized dirigible coming in to dock with the laboratory. It was a leather balloon with large wings on either side. The wings each had props to propel the ship forward. The gondola on the bottom was designed with wings that came out to look like eagle wings. They closed up against the gondola as it drew nearer to the plank. The props came to a stop as the ship settled on a pair of arms that extended up to it.

"Josh, are you awake?" Master Mel called out.

Josh left the window and raced out of his room and down a corridor, where he found Mel standing near a grand entrance.

"Good morning, Master Mel," Josh greeted him.

Mel spent a moment straightening out Josh's appearance. "You slept right through breakfast. I thought I told you to set the water clock to seven."

"I've never used a water clock before. I couldn't figure it out. I didn't want to wake you to ask."

"Remember, you are here to learn. Learning to be responsible is part of that. I expect you to not be late again. Now, we'll have tea with our guests, so you can have something to eat then."

"Who are the guests? That isn't an Imperial dirigible."

"It most certainly is not. That's the traveling balloon for Master Jeremiah. He's transporting Masters Netan and Ozias."

"Who are they?" Josh asked just as the door opened.

Three men stood there, the one in the front the oldest and most severe looking. Each wore elaborate suits with carefully sewn fine fabrics. Gold, brass, and silver buttons decorated their clothes as well as chains. Each had a long coat that came down to their knees or below. Top hats were on their heads with goggles, clocks, feathers, chains, cogs, gears, and other assorted metal objects. Two held exquisite canes decorated much as the rest of them with brass and bronze overlaid on the wooden shaft.

The two in the back were younger with cheerful smiles on their faces. The one in the front bore a long white beard and a single monocle on his face connected to a long chair.

The eldest sneered at Josh. "Who are we? What a smart-mouthed apprentice you have, Master Mel. Surely, you would have taught him about the other grand mages."

"Josh has only been my apprentice for one night," Mel answered kindly.

"Ah, I see. Well, young man, you will learn. I'm Master Jeremiah, the leader of the magi order."

Mel gestured to the others. "This is Ozias and Netan, the others of the order of the magi. Now"—he flicked open a pocket watch—"it's time for tea, which is waiting for us in my study."

After a long trip down to the bottom floor on the balloon, the group met for tea and treats while they spoke. Josh ate a plateful of cookies as he listened to the deep conversation between the four mages.

Jeremiah stood at the table, looking over the star charts. "It has been three years since it appeared in the skies, yet so few have noticed. It makes little sense to me."

Mel pointed at five open books on the table. "I've researched all the stellar phenomena in all my records and found nothing like this."

Master Ozias walked around the table, his cane tapping with his steps. "A new star in the heavens—and one that is the brightest any mage has ever recorded. Yet only a few can see it. How peculiar."

Netan poured himself a cup of tea. "My friends, it is as I have said. This is a sign from God."

Jeremiah stroked his long beard. "I was against such an interpretation for a long time. But there is so much about this that smacks of Divine nature. I've told you many times, there's a prophecy being fulfilled. The Judine Messiah has arrived, and this star is proof that He is of Divine origin. Many claimed to be messiahs over the centuries, but none had any Divine announcement."

Josh's interest was piqued. "Do you mean the Messiah of my people?"

Jeremiah huffed. "What is your apprentice saying?"

"My apprentice comes from the Judine province—at least, his family did," said Mel.

Jeremiah turned, that strict face staring at the nervous kid. "Ah, I see. Yes. We mages have kept the knowledge and histories of many peoples. The religious writings of many people are within our libraries and read by us. We search for their signs and prophecies to see what they mean. However, none have yet to produce such a clear fulfillment as this one. Come, let me show you." He waved a hand at the boy.

Josh got up and joined them. Jeremiah pulled over one of the scrolls Mel had been going through. Josh saw beautiful writing in a language he could not read. "What is this?"

"It's the writings of your people. This scroll is seven hundred years old and speaks of a Messiah Who would arrive in a town in the Judine provinces."

"Not at the temple or the capital city?" Josh asked.

"I don't know why the god of these people would choose such a place; but according to this prophecy, that is what he would choose. This star, which is strange by all accounts of known science, hangs in the sky, directing our attention to the Judine province. Recently, it has moved slightly, and we want to know what in the heavens could move a star or even place one to begin with. The prophecy tells of a Messiah rising there, and now a star that defies science that could be sent by a god hangs over that province. Furthermore, it is hidden from the eyes of the world, a world that mostly would detest such a Messiah." Jeremiah stood up and spoke to the others. "This star must be the guiding light to the Messiah."

"But, Jeremiah, why do our eyes see it alone? Surely, the god of these people would want to tell them first?" Master Netan asked.

"There could be others who can see it," said Mel. "I suspect there are Judine people who can see it. But I don't know where to find them or where this star is pointing us to."

"I suggest we go and ask," Said Master Ozias.

"Go where? The Judine province?" Mel asked.

"The prophecy speaks of a great king, one who would overthrow evil in this world," answered Ozias. "If this Messiah king is of the people of the Judine province, then we go there. The Judine's have a king; perhaps, he could help."

Jeremiah huffed. "You mean, a puppet to the emperor's governor."

"Still, if any would know of this prophecy and even perhaps the star, it should be them." Ozias picked up a cookie.

"I agree," said Mel. "Have you prepared for this visit, Master Jeremiah?"

The old man nodded. "I emptied our coffers. We have gold, rare perfumes, expensive lotions—all the regal gifts to offer such a king."

"What's with the gifts?" asked Josh.

"If we find this Messiah," explained Mel, "then he is of a veritable god. In all the time the mages have studied the religious texts and teachings of so many cultures, we have yet to come across a real fulfilled prophecy—no actual god in flesh, just words and beliefs. To meet a flesh-and-blood god sent to this world is to meet a king of kings. We, the mages, will offer our riches to this one and demonstrate that we acknowledge him as a real god. That is, of course, if this is all true."

Jeremiah rolled up the star charts. "Then, we must be on our way."

"First tea, then I'll get my ship ready." Mel sat down and poured himself a cup.

Jeremiah sat down. "Fine, tea time first. Then, we are on our way."

CHAPTER 5

JOSH HELPED GATHER BOOKS AND charts with his new master. The bookbags alone were so heavy that he had to drag them across the ground to get to the landing platform. He found the other masters with many cartons waiting at the dock, but no ship.

"Master Mel, where's the ship?"

Mel smiled. "We'll be taking my ship. Master Jeremiah's is too small for a trip such as this."

Jeremiah looked at his pocket watch. "Let's get this going."

Mel walked over to a wall near the dock and opened a panel. He put in his special key and turned it three times. He pulled down two levers and then pushed a third up. When the last lever was used, a great sound of metal gears and cogs turning came from under the water. The surface of the sea rumbled and boiled. A straight line formed in the water as two doors were lifted and then parted.

From within a hidden hangar bay came a massive airship. The body of the ship appeared like a great galleon made of wood and overlaid with many ornate metalwork designs. Windows dotted the outside, along with a few weapon ports. Where the sails would be were immense towers holding propellers that rattled and turned as they came alive. The roaring engines lifted the ship up out of the bay and toward the dock, perfectly aligning to let them board. A great tail spread out from the back like a fan, which would obviously direct the ship in the air as they moved along.

Mel laughed. "By that gaping mouth and those wide eyes, I suspect you haven't seen a ship quite like this, Josh."

"I've seen many glorious airships, but this one is beautiful. It's so . . . big."

"Master Mel's airship is the most spectacular of the magi," said Master Ozias.

"And the most powerful," added Netan.

Mel looked at his own pocket watch. "However, I don't believe we'll need any weapons on this journey. Let's get a move on, shall we?"

The masters and Josh hefted all the items onto the ship. The interior was just as marvelous, with gilded metal work all over the pristine wooden walls. It was like being in a mansion—at least, in Josh's mind.

Once they were all ready to go, Mel stood before the wheel. "Off we go."

He cranked back a large lever next to the wheel, and the engine sped up. Jets of steam spewed out of two large pipes on the back, and the ship lurched forward. The tail swung under the tender care of the wheel as Master Mel guided them away from his grand library.

Josh stood at the edge of the railing and laughed in jubilation. The world passed by below them, people gawking at the glorious ship above. The sky was as blue as he had ever seen, with gentle clouds rolling by.

Master Jeremiah drew up closer to Mel at the wheel. "The empire has a lot of presence around these cities here in the Iabera province; and they know better than to stop a magi ship, especially yours. However, there is less protection in the Judine provinces. We carry a lot of wealth, and this ship is a tempting target. Be mindful as we get closer."

"Don't worry, you old fusspot, the *Majesty* is the most powerful ship ever built by the magi. I doubt anyone would be foolish enough to raid us."

"Just warning you." Jeremiah shuffled away.

Josh came over. "Is he right? Are we in danger?"

"Don't worry. We're perfectly safe. Just enjoy yourself. I am taking you to your homeland. I think you would be more excited about that than worrying about what some old pessimist has to say."

Jeremiah let out an audible grunt at that comment.

Josh smiled. "I've wanted to see the temple in Sal Zi for many years."

"Then think of that and don't worry."

Master Ozias came over with a little box in his hand. "Come, young Josh, I would love to teach you some history while we enjoy the ride."

"Go with Master Ozias; learn." Mel shooed Josh away.

THE *MAJESTY* FLEW HARD THROUGH the day and into the night. Many other airships passed them, mostly military vessels from the empire. While Mel kept his confident attitude, it was worrisome the way the Imperials would watch them as they passed. Josh felt a lump in his stomach each time those soldiers would glare in their direction. However, none dared to stop them for inspection. They passed a few flying barges belonging to dignitaries and other wealthy people from around the provinces.

Josh stood at the edge of the railing, looking down at the passing farms and roads. The dark sky twinkled with millions of stars at this early hour of the morning.

"Josh, why are you up so early? Or have you not gone to bed?" Master Netan joined him.

Josh let out a heavy sigh. "I couldn't sleep. I'm sad."

"What about?"

"Master Ozias taught me about the history of the Judine people. They have been slaves to other nations repeatedly. Now, their land belongs to the empire, land that was given to them by God."

Netan nodded. "Ah, I see. Yes, the Judine people are a proud people with a troubled past. They have rebelled often against their oppressors and have faced much persecution for it. The empire does not trust them."

"All they want is to be free and live as God wanted them to. My parents were Judine, and they died because the empire hated my people so much."

Netan smiled. "Your people have spent centuries waiting for a leader who would free them from oppression. We hope this star tells us he has arrived. If this is true, this Messiah is not only supposed to free his chosen people but also bring peace to the entire world. So, there is hope, my young friend."

"I heard all the mages talking about some new star. What new star? How can you tell? There are so many?"

Netan frowned and cocked his head. "Do you not see it?"

"See what?"

Netan pointed out from the ship. "See, there, in the distance? There is a brilliant light in the sky— lower than any other known star. It shines down on the earth like a great beacon. Surely you can see this?"

Josh looked out with a deep frown. "I . . . I see nothing like that."

"How interesting."

Master Mel, standing at the helm, called out, "We have arrived at Sal Zi!"

James jumped up and looked at the passing land below them. A great city came into view. Half the city still had little lights dancing in the windows, while the other half was being covered by the rising sun. The buildings were close together, and all seemed to be made of the same sandy brown material. Cloth coverings were held up by poles in places to guard from the daylight. A vast network of cable lines spread out like a spiderweb across the city. These cables carried small gondolas that were moving along and then shifted one direction or another, sometimes lowering down to the ground and then returning to the network.

A magnificent structure rested in the middle of the town. It had two full courtyards, grand columns, and a central structure with people in priestly garments hurrying around.

Netan smiled and pointed. "That, my boy, is the temple. Isn't it beautiful?"

"Yes. Wow, Sal Zi . . . I always wanted to come here," Josh whispered.

"I have been here before. They are friendly people, but they hate the empire more than most and don't mind saying it—as long as there aren't many soldiers around," Netan said.

"My mother talked about her family coming here during the year for festivals and events," said Josh. "They would come to the temple to worship. I was brought here as an infant, but they died before I could come back when I would remember."

"They would be pleased you have had the chance."

Chapter 6

Mel maneuvered the ship toward the palace, flying low over the city. As they approached the palace, two men on the roof waved green flags at them, directing them to the airfield. In the field, a large wooden arm rose from the ground and met the ship at the side. Four more arms came up from under the ship and grabbed it to hold it in place. The engines were shut down, and they finally came to a stop.

Master Jeremiah led the other mages to the dock. Each had dressed in their finest suits and robes for the occasion. Josh followed Master Mel closely.

Jeremiah held up a hand to pause everyone while a group from the palace came to meet them. He whispered, "The apprentice should stay behind. He is not dressed for the occasion, nor is he trained in how to act."

Mel put a hand on Josh's shoulder. "My apprentice looks fine, and he knows to keep his mouth shut."

Jeremiah let out a heavy sigh, but he did not further protest since their greeters had arrived.

The men in flowing robes with long tassels on all the corners stopped and bowed. The man at the front said, "King Herod welcomes the mages to his palace."

Jeremiah bowed to them. "We apologize for not announcing our visit before arriving."

"Not to worry, Master Mage. Your presence is always welcome. Come with me."

The greeters led them down the dock and into the palace. Josh noted how ancient this place was compared to Mel's library. There were steam pipes running through areas, and most of the doors were properly controlled by cogs. But much of the building was stone and wood, not metal. He was surprised by the many draping fabrics hanging from the walls.

"You have pretty fabrics," Josh said, which drew a glare from Jeremiah.

The lead greeter answered, "One of our many exports is finely woven fabrics. The tapestries here are all hand-dyed and then woven by master artisans. Would you like a fine outfit of woven fabric, young man?"

Mel almost answered with a no, but Jeremiah interrupted. "It would be our pleasure to accept such a gift. Josh, go with the servant. Now."

Josh was painfully aware this was how Jeremiah was getting rid of him before meeting the king, but he wouldn't protest.

A kind woman ushered him away and down a long hallway. He was brought into a room full of fabrics. Three old ladies laughed and spoke around him in the old language of the Judine people. He couldn't understand them. He spent his time looking at the incredible fabrics.

"What color do you like?" the young lady who had escorted him asked.

He looked at the fabrics and felt a growing sense of sadness in him. He knew some of these patterns and colors; his mother and father had worn them. He touched a blue sash. "I like this. My mother once wore something like this."

This caused a stir among the ladies. One older lady asked, "Are you of the Binin Clan?"

"Binin?" He frowned. "Yes, my great grandfather was Binin Josh. I'm named after him; but my full name is Tal Josh, since that was the name the Imperials gave my father's family when they moved them."

"Oh, your father was Tal. Then he was originally part of the Binin Clan as well. You are Judine."

"Yes. I am. But I know little about my history."

The ladies all gathered up parts for a new outfit. The eldest said, "We will dress you in your ancestors' colors and styles. Praise God, we love to see a child of God return to his home."

After a flurry of clothing changes, he was finally dressed. He rarely wore such nice clothing and never any in this style. However, he liked it. He wore pants and a shirt that was ecru and blue with silver buttons. Tassels hung from the corners of the shirt. Over that, he had a long duster with a thick hood and wide sleeves. The coat had a golden chain that draped around the waist. Around his neck hung a special set of goggles with heavily tinted glass for moving about in the bright, arid climate.

Once dressed, he was escorted back to where the other masters waited. He found all the mages sitting on pillows in a room filled with more pillows, draping fabrics, and an elegant tea set out on a low table. However, he did not see anyone else besides the masters.

"Back so soon?" inquired Jeremiah.

"They were quick," Josh answered.

"Josh, you look amazing!" Mel waved him over.

Josh walked in and turned around once. "I love this. It's so comfortable."

"It needs one thing." Mel pulled out a pocket watch and handed it to him.

"I can't take your watch."

"Of course, you can. I have three." Mel held out two more from different pockets.

"Enough of this. Why are we waiting?" Jeremiah looked at his own watch.

The main doors opened, and a servant bowed to them as he announced, "His Majesty, King Herod."

A younger man in elegant robes strode in with a small entourage of servants. He tilted his head toward his guests. "Welcome to my palace, Master Mages. I am eager to speak with you."

The mages all stood and bowed in his direction.

Master Jeremiah said, "It is our honor to be your guest, King of Sal Zi."

"Sit. Have some tea. Let us speak." King Herod swept around the room and sat on a glorious golden pillow that allowed him to be half-a-foot higher than the others. One of his servants poured him a cup of tea and handed it to him. "I have been awaiting your visit, my friends."

The mages all looked at each other with quizzical gazes.

Herod obviously noticed their curiosity. "No, none of the mages here have sent me any correspondence. My own sages have seen your arrival."

Mel said, "I did not realize you had diviners here."

"My sages are not like a true mage. They do not see the future or have fantastic powers. However, they're wise and listen to the common rabble. Two years ago, the murmurs began about a star in the East, a symbol of the fabled Messiah. Since then, the noise among the peasants has only grown stronger. A day does not pass without someone claiming to have heard of the Messiah coming here or there.

However, what has been most disturbing is a growing segment of my people have claimed to see this star in the East. I cannot see this, and my sages cannot find any astrological experts who can see it; so I'm understandably concerned."

"It sounds as if you do not believe these rumors of a star or Messiah," said Master Netan.

"I dismissed this as another hoax, another episode of mass hysteria. Over the centuries, there have been many claims of the Messiah walking among us; and they all have proven to be false. I believed this to be just as false. I was more concerned with what my people would do. I fear they might lift some rebel leader against the empire. Convince the common rabble that he is the Messiah and start a revolt that could get us all killed by the Legions."

"Forgive me, but what does this have to do with our arrival?" Mel asked.

"Until you showed up, I was willing to dismiss this as a mere hoax. But when my servants told me you were here to speak with me about a star in the East, I am now certain it is true. It might have finally happened, and the fabled Messiah has arrived."

"We'd hoped you already had information about this," said Master Jeremiah. "We're on a journey to find him ourselves. It is . . . strange that you do not see this star, but we can."

"I'm afraid I cannot, and my own sages and scientists are blind to it as well. I cannot say why. However, we know a general direction which the people seem to believe it is pointing—East. Do you have an actual location?"

Master Ozias said, "We have seen it; but at a great distance, it's hard to be clear on this."

"Then may I ask a favor of you? The Judine people have long desired to meet their Messiah. Could you find him and then return to me and let me know where he is? I would like to escort him back here for the people."

"Then he can become King of the Judine people like the prophecy said!" exclaimed Josh.

Herod had a thin smile on his face at this. "Yes, of course."

"It would be our honor to help," said Master Jeremiah. "First, we have to find him."

"Then, by all means, ask what you need; and I shall provide it for your journey."

Jeremiah bowed his head. "How gracious."

CHAPTER 7

JOSH WALKED WITH MASTER MEL through the busy markets of Sal Zi. People from all over the Judine province mingled as they bartered and traded.

"What are we doing out here?" Josh asked.

Mel let a man pass them. "We need to find people who have seen the star. They can help us find a path to it."

"I still don't know what you are talking about. I haven't seen a special star at night."

Mel stepped onto a trolley connected to the vast cable system. Mel said, "I cannot say why you don't see it. But we know it's there."

A man on the trolley leaned over and whispered, "Follow me. I know of the star."

The trolley lowered back to the ground, and they stepped off. Josh noticed Mel had a hand inside his vest, holding an electro-pistol.

All three stopped at a booth; and the man held them back, pausing their approach.

A woman at the booth was in tears as a man dressed in Imperial clothing stood with a small child next to him. He had a hand out to the woman. "I told you, if you don't want me telling the soldiers about your connection to the rebellion, you'll have to pay double taxes."

"But we aren't connected to any rebellion," she protested. "And I don't have that kind of money."

He leaned in. "Would be a shame to send you to prison."

Opening a box, she emptied all the cash into his open hand. "Is that enough?"

He laughed at his haul. "Good enough. Try to have more next time. Come on, Matt; we have more taxes to collect."

The man with Mel and Josh muttered, "Horrible tax collectors are bleeding us dry. That one is the worst scum of them and is training his son to be just like him—both traitors to their own people."

After the tax collector and his child left, Mel and Josh were brought over to the fruit stand. The man greeted his wife. "Are you okay?"

"He didn't hurt me, just scared me. Took all our money."

"We'll survive. This man was asking about the star."

She tensed up. "Are you with the empire?"

Mel tipped his hat to her. "No, ma'am, I'm a mage doing research with my apprentice. If you don't feel comfortable telling me about the star, I can leave."

"Oh, a mage. Wow. No, please, come, come!" She and her husband led them behind a building. Five other people were there, cleaning and drying clothes.

"These are our friends and family," said the man. "We all have seen the star and are waiting on the Messiah."

An elderly man smiled at Josh. "A Binin boy. I haven't met you before."

"I, uh, just got here."

Mel stepped forward. "We don't have a lot of time. Anything you can tell us about this star would be helpful. Its location is important."

The old man looked around and waved them closer. "It appeared one night, but none of us saw it—only shepherds in the fields near Bet'la. They told us about it, and we all started seeing it."

The fruit-stand woman shook her head. "Some of us. Some still don't see it."

"Where was it spotted?" Mel asked, pulling out a little notebook from inside his vest.

An old woman, wringing out some pants from the wash, said, "Look to the fields where they graze the sheep outside Bet'la."

Mel scribbled that down. "Good to know. Anything else?"

Imperial soldiers came rushing around corners and down the alley. Each had electro-rifles ready to fire. A commander stepped up and aimed a gun at the man who helped them. "Binin Hir, you're under arrest for rebel activity."

"What! We aren't rebels!"

The man smiled. "I don't care. You've been found talking about the rebel leader calling himself the Messiah. That's enough to convict you."

"He is here. I'm just saying he is here! I'm not rebelling!"

The commander laughed. "Enough talk." He jerked and gagged and then fell down. His soldiers all did the same.

Mel tightened his glove from where he had just thrown tiny electro pellets at them. "I would get away from here quickly. They'll wake in an hour. Do nothing to them; just flee."

"Thank you. God bless you." The old woman hesitated.

"No time. Move." Mel waved her off and then ran with Josh in a different direction. They rounded a corner and jumped onto the nearest trolley lift.

Josh caught his breath. "That was amazing."

Mel kept out a keen eye as they traveled along the complex trolley system. "Normally, mages are not to interfere too much. But I couldn't allow them to be taken away. They were no danger."

Josh looked over the edge of the trolley down to the streets below. "Soldiers are everywhere, picking on people. Tax collectors are stealing their money. The Messiah couldn't come soon enough to stomp the empire into the dust."

Mel watched the trolley shift cables as it headed for the royal palace. "Be careful of your words and attitude toward the empire until we leave. King Herod reports to the emperor, and I don't want anyone knowing what we just did."

"I understand."

THE NEXT MORNING, THE MAGI and Josh bid farewell to the king and set sail across the skies over Sal Zi, heading east. The events of the day before still burned in the heart and mind of Josh, his hatred of the empire growing as he recalled the unfair treatment of the Judine people in their own city.

"Master, could the mages stop the empire?" Josh asked while his master piloted the ship.

"Our technology is far superior to the empire's, but our resources are far weaker. Besides, it's the duty of the mages to remain outside the events of other nations, only guiding through wisdom and recording for historical records. We're knowledge-keepers and seekers, not generals or commanders, and certainly not usurpers. Let history write itself. We'll just watch it unfold."

"I hope we find the Messiah," Josh said wistfully.

Mel seemed amused. "Why the sudden urge?"

"I'm gonna tell Him what happened and what's going on and about my parents. I want Him to fulfill prophecy and defeat the empire and throw them out of the Judine province."

"Careful of letting the desire for revenge cloud your emotions."

Josh frowned. "I want justice."

"Is that your only reason? Justice? Don't answer me; just think hard about it as we head out."

Master Ozias came running from the aft section. "Master Mel, we have company."

"Raiders?"Ozias shook his head. "No. Three Imperial craft just lifted off from the military base outside Sal Zir and are following us. They fly the flag of the empire and the Judine flag."

"Ah, an escort. I suspected Herod wouldn't let us do this alone."

"He wants to find the Messiah, too." Josh looked anxiously behind him as though expecting to see the Imperial soldiers.

"Let's hope it is for the right reasons," Mel said.

CHAPTER 8

JOSH SAW HIS WORLD FROM a shorter perspective. He was lying on the floor in a home. Two people stood over him, smiling and talking to him. He couldn't understand the words, but he could hear the voice.

"Mom? Dad?" He reached up and found his tiny, infant hand being played with by the gentle fingers of his mother.

"But you're dead." The moment he said this, his world changed to the moment he had found his home in ruins and two bodies being carried out by local authorities. They were coming to take him to a foster home, so he ran as hard as he could, crying.

Sitting up with a gasp of air, he realized he had been dreaming. The throbbing of his heart and wetness on his cheeks made it feel so real. The cool night air and thrumming of the engines oriented him to reality.

"Josh?" Master Jeremiah found him sleeping on the deck. "If you want to sleep, go to your cabin."

Josh stood up. "Sorry. I nodded off."

"Don't worry. You woke in time. We are approaching the pasturelands near Bet'la. Come, you must see this."

Josh got up and followed Master Jeremiah to where the other masters stood. All were in awe of something he could not see.

"Master Mel? Are we there yet?"

Mel looked out. "Can you not see the star? It's so close. I've never seen such a beautiful sight."

Josh gazed out with a deeply furrowed brow. "All I see is a little town in the distance."

Ozias pointed toward a distant town. "Over that town is a glorious star. This has to be Divine."

"Come, let us get there quickly." Jeremiah waved at Mel.

Mel returned to the wheel with Josh next to him. Josh looked behind the ship. "Those other ships are still following us."

"They have moved no closer, just stayed at the same distance," Mel said.

Jeremiah turned to look back. "I'm concerned about that. I feel our friend, King Herod, might not trust us."

"I don't know what he's up to. As long as they stay far enough back, we'll be fine." Mel pushed a lever forward, and the steam jets pushed harder.

Shepherds hurried along their flocks as they gawked at the massive ship flying lower over the fields. Finally, the shadow of the *Majesty* nearly covered the tiny town of Bet'la. The few people out at this late hour paused in awe of the ship.

"Taking us down for a landing," Mel called out.

Josh held on tightly as the *Majesty* lowered down in the nearest field. Small ports opened under it, and landing struts came out. The ship sank down on the wooden struts, and the engines came to a stop.

All the mages took up boxes of their presents and made their way to a side door. Once it opened, a series of steps formed from an extended metal platform. They walked down and headed into town.

"The other ships are waiting," Netan said.

Mel glanced back. "Let them wait. We'll do what we came to do."

Josh kept up with Mel as they headed into town. "So, do you know where we're going?"

"Nope. Just following the starlight."

Josh looked around. "Are you sure a great king would be here? This is a pitiful little town."

"All signs have pointed us here. I admit it is a strange place for a king to be found." Mel said.

"When we find this Man, will you let Him use your ship to return to Sal Zi?"

"If he asks, I won't mind escorting him."

Josh was practically giddy. "What about letting Him use it for the war?"

"War? Now you are really getting ahead of yourself."

Josh frowned. "Do I smell bread baking? It's so early in the morning."

Ozias answered, "Bet'la is known as the House of Bread. They have provided bread for much of the Judine province for centuries. It's a fine smell, better than the smell of sheep that comes in on the breezes."

"Look, my friends. The light shines on that old farm—behind it!" Jeremiah called out.

Josh felt his heart pounding and his energy racing. He was eager to meet the hero who would avenge his parents. "Come on!" He ran ahead.

"Josh!" Mel called out in vain.

The masters rounded the old farm and found a pasture behind it with a small tower of stone. A woman held her young son while pouring water into a trough when they saw the group heading toward them.

"Joe!"

A man with a shepherd's crook came up quickly from a nearby field.

Josh had already spied the man and was ready to meet this new Messiah. However, his masters all looked at her and then the young boy.

"Master Mel, there he is!" Josh pointed at the man with the crook.

The masters fell to their knees and bowed, placing the boxes in their hands before them. Master Jeremiah said, "We have come to worship the one true Messiah, Son of God most High."

Josh looked at the man and then at the boy.

Voices sang out around him, "The son of God, God made flesh. Praise be to God, Who comes to defeat death. Glory to God in the highest, And on earth peace, goodwill toward men!"[1]

In this moment, Josh finally understood the prophecies his mother had told him. God wasn't sending a military leader; God was sending Himself. The enemy wasn't the empire; it was death itself. All at once, the surrounding field grew bright with a pure light. He looked up and saw the star. It did not hurt his eyes; it filled him with hope. Josh fell to his knees and then put his face to the ground before the Child.

Josh had tears running down his face onto the ground. He felt so guilty for having completely misunderstood everything. Yet he also felt anger that he would not see the Messiah command armies that would overthrow the empire and get revenge.

While he had his face down, weeping in sorrow, a gentle hand touched his back; and he heard a voice say,

"'You shall not take vengeance, nor bear any grudge against the children of your people, but you shall love your neighbor as yourself: I *am* the LORD.'"[2]

---

1 Luke 2:14, New King James Version
2 Leviticus 19:18, New King James Version

Josh looked up and found that small Child simply smiling at him, still in His mother's arms.

Then came a great flash of light from the star and a being wearing bright clothes stood before them. "Go, flee this place. Do not return the way you came, Magi. The one who asked you to return did so out of great evil. Joe, take your wife and the Son of God and flee to the land of Anu, where Herod cannot touch you. Go now!"

The light faded completely, the star vanishing from the sky.

"Joe?" The mother held her child closer to her and looked at her husband.

Mel stood up and bowed his head to them. "Come with me. We can take you from here. The enemy is at your door now."

CHAPTER 9

THE MAGES AND JOSH HELPED the young family gather what little they had and fled to the *Majesty*. The ships from Herod remained waiting out in the field as the sun slowly rose on the horizon.

Master Mel ran to the helm and began the disembarking procedures. Netan activated a communication station near the helm.

"Can you link into their systems?" Mel asked.

"I think so."

Jeremiah pulled over cables from a different system. "I can rewire it to intercept them."

Mel pulled up a cone from the dash beside him. "Ozias, prepare the smoke canisters."

The family of the Messiah stood on the top deck, bracing themselves as the ship rattled into the air. Josh ran down to comfort them.

"It's gonna be all right. They're the mages; they're fantastic at what they do."

Joe looked calmly back at Josh. "I know we'll be safe. God is good."

Josh felt a small hand grab his. The feel of the tiny fingers were like his own in his dream from the night before. The Boy, the Messiah, held his hand by two fingers. There was a sense of safety and comfort that overwhelmed him.

Josh smiled. "It's going to be all right."

The *Majesty* lurched hard and turned in the air over the city. Four aft cannons came out from the ship and blasted out the smoking canisters. Each one hit the ground in the distant pastures and erupted in clouds of thick smoke. With a hard thrust forward, the ship sped away from Bet'la before their enemy could make it through the cloud.

Mel called out, "Did they see us?"

Netan watched a screen on the glass monitor. Voices from the enemy ships came through, talking to each other. He gave a thumbs-up. "They were taken completely by surprise. They do not know where we've gone."

"Perfect. Hold on. We're going to be moving fast for a while." Mel pushed forward on the lever, and the ship sped up even faster.

Josh smiled at the family in front of him. "It's all over."

"Wait! I'm getting something," Netan called out, then went silent.

"Don't keep it to yourself!" Jeremiah yelled.

Netan looked up, his face drained of color. "Herod has contacted the enemy ships. He . . . he just ordered Bet'la destroyed."

"No." Josh stood up just as an orange fireball rose into the sky. The sound of cannon fire and electro-charges echoed across the plains.

Mel slammed a fist against his wheel. "We should never have stopped in Sal Zi!"

"We could not have known what he would do," said Jeremiah.

"I always knew Herod was a power-hungry puppet of the empire," said Mel. "But I didn't know he was this bloodthirsty. I thought his heritage would have some impact on his life."

Ozias turned to the small group. "There is little we can do now. We have the Messiah. Let's get him to safety."

The sun sat over the waters of the sea near the port of Xandry in the province of Anu. The *Majesty* now floated in the water, a plank connecting it to the dock. The family of the Messiah were put on a cart with their meager belongings and the gifts of the magi. They bid farewell and rode off into a new land far from home.

Josh watched them leave. "Master, how could I have been so wrong?"

"We always want revenge for the wrongs against us. It is not wrong to want justice, but justice is only made perfect when applied with righteousness. None of us are truly righteous."

"But He isn't even in his homeland!"

"And He is a child when we expected a man. At this point, I think we need to put faith in God's plan."

Josh watched that small Boy leaving with His parents. "I've seen the face of God; He has come to us as a mere child. Yet somehow, it brings me the most fantastic feeling of hope to know He is finally here."

"Hope. That is exactly what I feel as well."

"I want to study the words of God, but I'm afraid to go back to Judine," admitted Josh.

Mel smiled. "Then it's a good thing that my library holds copies of all the writings of the Judine people. Let's go home, and you can study the words of the Lord. Perhaps, when the time comes that the Messiah fully reveals Himself, you will be ready to follow."

"Let's go home."

THE AMNESTY RULE

Lauren Smyth

CHAPTER 1

What surprised me most about war is how uninteresting it is. I have been at the front for three weeks; and when I arrived, I was given a clumsy rifle and a box of cartridges and told to assist the soldiers or get out of the way. As far as I can tell, I have done neither. Yet I haven't been sent home because everyone understands that there is nothing to do.

I have chewed through three pencils trying to think of a story. I could write about how war is squalid, rotten, producing battlefields that reek of decay and trenches ankle-deep in garbage—more of the same sensational stories that are already circulating en masse. My editors would devour it like thirsty dogs and feed it to the public faster than the government can churn out soldiers.

But though this would not be a lie, it would be far from the actual soldier's experience. Doubtless, war is the creator of extensive misery. Most of that misery, however, falls on those who are left at home. The soldiers—popularly supposed to be charging machine gun embankments and screaming battle songs and diving into holes to avoid the bombs dropped by godless, virtue-less, moral-less enemies—are playing cards and cracking jokes that would make a seaman blush. No one has thought to provide entertainment

because war is supposed to be entertainment enough. But the
front, which is popularly supposed to be right outside our tents,
is nowhere to be found.

—November 25, 1940

"I'm a journalist, not a soldier. What's more, I'm a pacifist. Why should I carry a weapon when I don't intend to fight?"

The corporal took a lazy drag of his cigar. "You don't have to shoot if you don't want to. But you will." He began to cackle, working himself up from a preliminary snort to a full-bellied chortling that made the windowpanes—and the journalist—shiver. "Just you wait until you find yourself on the wrong end of someone else's rifle. You'll be glad we gave you a gun then; and you'll use it, too, whether you're a pacifist or an anarchist or any other 'ist.' Just you wait!"

"But my principles—"

"The enemy could care less about your principles." The corporal waved him aside with a flick of his cigar. "You strike me as feeble for your profession. Excuse me, but I'll be seeing your papers."

A slight flicker in the journalist's eyes was the only indication that his pacifism was trickling away like rain through a drainpipe. He unfolded his papers and handed them across the desk to the corporal, who flicked the ash off his cigar onto the journalist's neat coat.

"Rolf Allard." He sneered. "A German first name and a French last name. A dirty half-breed, eh?"

"My mother was German, and my father was French, if that's what you're asking."

"Forbidden love, I see." The corporal, French both in nationality and spirit, nodded approvingly. "Aged twenty-six, writer for *La Liberté*—hein, that newspaper is all my cousin reads, he'd love to meet you—born in Nice, raised in Paris. So, you are almost French."

"I am French."

"Well, then, everything seems to be in order." The corporal returned Rolf's papers decorated here and there with specks of ash. "Have a good day, Mr. Writer."

"You haven't answered my question about the rifle."

A hot wind of cigar smoke belched from the corporal's mouth. "You can help the soldiers, or you can drag yourself back to the home front and write about the New York pigeons dropping little white gifts in the politicians' hats. Journalism, my foot! Since when has the profession been this . . . so . . . " He whirled his hand wildly around his head. "Get out! Out!"

Chapter 2

It's remarkable what a man will do if you can convince him he is doing it for someone else rather than to satiate his own selfish greed. It proves that the spirit of generosity is alive, even in the worst of men. I, too, am guilty of this kind of well-intentioned insanity, or else I should not be in the middle of this disaster. Good intentions are worthless, indeed.

—December 9, 1940

"What's your accent from?"

"It's English," Rolf answered.

There was a choked ripple of laughter.

"So, you're a writer. An English writer, even worse!" said yet another soldier who looked like all the rest, down to his oily brown hair and exceedingly thick eyebrows. At least, he had a kindly crinkle about his eyes, although he did not smile; and he had the kind of face that suggested he did not intend to try. "Are you the kind of writer who boosts morale or the kind who tells it like he sees it?"

"I'd like to think I'm both."

"Impossible. This is war."

"Then, I'd rather tell the truth."

"Telling the truth and telling it like you see it are different things."
But the man seemed satisfied with Rolf's answer, for he offered a
cigarette, which Rolf declined. "I'm Major Auclair. You'll get to know
the others once you've been with the battalion for a while. That kid
behind you is Desrosiers. He can show you around. Would you like to
unpack? What did you bring besides notebooks and"—he glanced at
Rolf's uniform—"a flat iron?"

"A rifle. Ammunition. But I don't want them. I'm a writer, not a
soldier, and I don't intend to fight."

"Leave them here." Auclair pointed to something that might once
have been a wine barrel. The top had since been hacked off, leaving
behind a jagged edge and a rusty forest of bayonets. "Someone else
will use them if you don't, but you'll change your mind. Want a drink?"

Someone forced a dusty beer bottle into Rolf's hand. He uncorked it
and took a cautious sniff. His eyes lit up, and he flipped the bottom up
and gulped the rest. One of the soldiers, who had been watching him
from behind a munitions truck, handed him another with a dry chuckle.

"Where are you from?" asked Desrosiers. He was a slight, pale-
faced boy with abundant freckles who looked just about old enough,
Rolf thought, to make a decent paperboy. He snatched Rolf's knapsack
out of his hands with unexpected energy, slung it over his back, and
marched toward the closest building. "I'll show you where to put your
kit and find a blanket."

The façade towering above Rolf's head casting a harsh shadow
over the street seemed to be all that remained of what had once been
an upscale apartment building or perhaps a hotel. From the outside,
it appeared to be about four stories tall, made of hard brownstone
from top to bottom and graced with a gray marble staircase that led

to a white front door. Debris and dust on the floor grated under Rolf's boots as he followed Desrosiers inside. The tile was cracked now, worn by hurrying feet; but it had once been smooth marble, and traces of the original sparkled through the grime. The wallpaper hung off the walls in uneven shreds. It was still relatively clean, and Rolf could tell it would have been sprinkled with soft pink roses and vines if the patterns were whole. It gave the room a soft, feminine air, which would have been comforting had it not been so ruthlessly violated.

Desrosiers led him up a creaky wooden staircase to the third floor, down a yellow-carpeted hall, and into a boxy room that overlooked the street. He dropped Rolf's knapsack in the closest corner, disturbing what Rolf realized with horror might have been a scorpion and sending it scuttling into a nearby vent. Desrosiers, incurious, stretched his shoulders and groaned.

"What's in that bag?" he demanded, massaging his biceps. "It's heavy!"

"Paper." Rolf tore his gaze from the vent, distracted by something moving in the street. "What's that?"

Desrosiers peeked around his arm, too short to see over his shoulder. "A deserter, I suppose." He whistled. "Poor fellow."

"But he's coming toward us."

"A deserter from *them*."

The man was sprinting like he could feel the dogs biting his heels, though from what Rolf could see, no one was chasing him. The street was so empty and silent that Rolf could almost hear his footsteps pounding and hard, rushed and rhythmic—like the beating of the soldiers' drums. The city was holding its breath, waiting to see how far he would get.

"Don't you know? They've got the Mauser—" A crack interrupted Desrosiers's shrill voice. The man tripped over his own feet, staggering into the corner of a building. Rolf ran to the window and pushed it open. The iron window guard shook as he leaned over it. He glimpsed the man disappearing below him, reeling into the arms of the French sentry, hands clutching his stomach.

Another crack and the whizz of bullet chipping off stone.

"Mauser Karabiner," Desrosiers continued patiently. "That's a German-made long-distance rifle. More accurate than ours."

"They must be close." Rolf closed the shutters.

"How far away did you think they were?" Desrosiers laughed. "What good would rifles be if we couldn't hit each other?"

"Couldn't we surround them if they're so close?" Rolf murmured, dusting paint chips from the window off his hands. "Throw a grenade, kill them all, have this whole mess over within a day."

"Not unless you want to be the one waltzing down the street with no cover. Good luck trying to guess which building is empty and which one is hiding snipers," interrupted Auclair's husky voice from the hallway. "One of them could defend the place against fifty of us. The streets are narrow and the houses close together. Who'd take those odds?"

"Not I." Desrosiers crossed himself. "What do you want to see, Journalist? I was going to show you something . . . "

"Where did that deserter go?"

"Oh, the blanket! You can have this one." Desrosiers handed Rolf a rough, moth-eaten piece of fabric reminiscent of a horse blanket. "Will this do? It doesn't matter, since that's all we have."

Rolf turned back to the window, trying to peek through the cracks in the shutters. "Shouldn't we find out what happened to the deserter?"

"Are you looking for a story?" Desrosiers began, but Rolf had already pushed past Auclair and was sprinting down the hallway.

In the street, he shoved his way through a crowd of silent soldiers circling the munitions truck, hissing apologies for trampled feet and bruised shoulders, until he spotted the deserter propped against the huge tire. The man's arms were still wrapped around his stomach; and his face, pale and soaked with sweat, was squeezed in agony. A soldier with a Red Cross badge on his shoulder was kneeling beside him, a bloody towel draped across his hands.

"I'm nearly done," he assured the deserter. "Don't make any more noise. Don't let them know you made it, or they'll toss a grenade over the barrier and kill us all."

The deserter whimpered something in Italian.

"You." The medic pointed at Rolf. "Get me some alcohol."

Rolf handed him the remains of his drink, but the medic shook his head. "Stronger. Whiskey. Vodka."

Rolf glanced helplessly at the soldiers behind him. They mumbled to each other; and a few of them glanced around as though the alcohol might suddenly appear out of thin air, but no one moved.

"Ah, these idiots. They don't know where to look. Come here and hold pressure on the wound. I'll find it myself." He tossed the towel at Rolf, who caught it automatically, and vanished around the front of the truck.

"Excuse me." Rolf wrang out the towel, dripping blood into the dusty cobbles. "He'll be back soon, I'm sure." He placed the towel over the place where there seemed to be the most blood. His patient's mouth opened in a silent shriek as he applied pressure. "Perhaps you don't speak English. Perhaps . . . Italian?" Rolf reattempted his apology, and the man's eyes shot open.

"*Voi*," he mumbled, pointing at Rolf's face. "You . . . I know. Voice."

Rolf smiled faintly. "I'm afraid that's all I know how to say."

"*Anche voi?*" He choked, and a stream of blood spilled out of his mouth.

"Medic!" Rolf tried to wipe the man's face clean with the towel, but the blood was replaced as fast as he mopped it. "Please, someone, help!"

The soldiers murmured in sympathy.

"Get the medic over here!" Rolf pressed his towel over the deserter's mouth.

The crowd rustled and shifted, and the medic staggered up with a wooden crate on his shoulder. "Why are you holding that towel up there? It's his stomach that's bleeding." He ripped the towel out of Rolf's grasp and whistled. "What's the use of wasting booze on a hopeless case?" he grumbled, uncorking a bottle of absinthe. "Infection won't kill him if he bleeds to death first."

"Isn't there anything you can do?"

The medic shrugged. "I suppose I could pray. Beyond that—"

"I don't believe in prayer. I believe in people."

"Isn't it too bad that people sometimes aren't good enough?" The deserter's head lolled forward against the medic's arm, and he snapped, "Hold him up! I can't see what I'm doing."

A vague rustle of noise erupted from behind Rolf, and he turned to see the crowd of soldiers parting to make room for a team of nurses with a stretcher. He tried to help, but they were more experienced than he. Before he could blink, they had carted the deserter away, leaving nothing behind to show he had been there but a few drops of blood and a torn strip of cloth from his uniform.

"Italian, eh?" someone remarked, shaking his head. "I thought we were fighting Germans."

"So did I." Rolf wobbled as he pulled himself to his feet.

"Are you all right?" the closest soldier asked, steadying him. "Ah, but you're a journalist. You've seen nothing yet." He grinned. "What's one wounded enemy compared to a whole great battle?"

"Or war," another voice added cheerfully.

"You'll get used to it," continued the soldier, slapping Rolf's back with a vigor that made the journalist flinch. "Hey, drink up! Alcohol's the one thing we have in abundance." He plucked a bottle of vodka from the medic's crate and pushed it into Rolf's hands. "Come on, man, drink!"

CHAPTER 3

Rifles are unbearably loud when you hear only one fired at a time. It is a different story when you hear twenty. "Loud" is the wrong word to describe them then; their reports are so overwhelming that your senses cannot take them in at all, and so you are left with nothing—no perception, no discomfort, only some ringing in your ears that may go away in a few days.

—December 10, 1940

Something silky caressed Rolf's face. He tossed and turned until he couldn't stand it, and then he wiped the back of his hand across his cheek. It came away white. A thin rain of plaster trickled down from the ceiling, burning his eyes. He didn't even bother to sigh as he unrolled himself from his blanket. This was, after all, the life he'd signed up for.

The building trembled. Rolf dove under a broken desk in the corner, closely followed by a groggy Desrosiers.

"What's that?" the boy was mumbling, rubbing his eyes, but Rolf grabbed his arm and yanked him back against the wall. Desrosiers barely managed to yelp, "Ouch!" before a beam smashed the floor where he had been crouching.

"Can you hear me?" Rolf shouted, his voice scratching his throat.

But he spoke too late. The battle had begun. Whistles and bangs and gunshots—those were the only noises he could identify with certainty—drowned out his exhausted voice. Desrosiers cupped his hand around his ear, and Rolf roared, "Get out of the building before it collapses!"

They scrambled out from under the desk through a thick fog of dust and bolted for the stairs. Rolf blundered into Desrosiers' back and nearly sent them pitching down faces first, but the boy grabbed the handrail and steadied them both. The steps creaked and swayed under their feet. Rolf scraped his elbow against the rough stone wall and shouted a curse, but he couldn't hear himself over the roaring noise. He thought Desrosiers said something. He put his foot out to take another step and tripped over the unexpectedly flat floor.

"Do you know how to shoot?" Desrosiers screamed in Rolf's ear. "Here, take this!" He pushed a rifle into Rolf's hands and disappeared around the corner of the munitions truck.

Rolf's fingers clenched tightly around the barrel of the rifle. He stared at the smooth wood and metal, then opened and closed the bolt. The action was smooth as silk, delicate and familiar under his fingers. He retrieved a pocket of ammunition from the metal canister beside the barrel and chambered the first cartridge.

Auclair happened to be in his sights when he raised the rifle to his shoulder. He was about thirty yards away; but Rolf could see him clearly, pointing at something in the distance and yelling inaudibly to a machine gunner behind a wall of sandbags. He was standing straight and tall, his back perfectly aligned in the aperture. Rolf breathed deeply, shifting his weight to his toes. The sight bobbed up, then down; and when it came to rest, Auclair had vanished.

Rolf shouldered the rifle and ran toward the south barricade. He saw the back of Desrosiers' white-haired head silhouetted against a half-destroyed wall; and with a running start, he dropped to his knees and coasted across the dirty street cobbles, coming to rest in a puddle beside Desrosiers' boots.

"What are we shooting at?" he shouted, tugging Desrosiers' sleeve. All he got for answer was a vigorous wave in the general direction beyond the barricade, so he pulled himself to his feet and peeked over the wall.

Before he could see anything more than a misty cloud, Desrosiers seized his arm and dragged him down. "Are you crazy?" he shrieked. "They'll shoot you!"

"Who's 'they'?" Rolf yelled back. But Desrosiers was busy again, and he got no answer.

Rolf edged his body along the ground until he could just barely see around the corner of the wall. With his rifle pressed against the side of his face, he waited until he could see something—a shadow or a movement, though he wasn't sure exactly what he expected—in the aperture of his sight.

He took a deep breath; and with a gentle pull, the rifle sprang back against his shoulder, and the shadow disappeared.

His lips were dry; and when he licked them, he found his tongue, too, was covered with dust. He couldn't yell a warning to Desrosiers when the boy tried to squeeze past him and run to the other side of the barricade. *No, you fool, the muzzle flashed; they've seen us now!*

He tried to grab Desrosiers' ankle, but he was too slow. The boy ran out into the open, five steps—or was it four? Rolf couldn't understand how he had time to think about it; and then Desrosiers was down, his mouth opening in a cry of pain that nobody could hear.

Rolf raised his rifle over his head and over the barricade and fired a few shots that, for all he knew, flew over the enemies' heads. It was the noise and the dust that mattered. He fired again, this time aiming his rifle at the ground, idiotically hoping to kick up a cloud of dust that would cover him. And then, without thinking, without even stopping to acknowledge that this was something he had sworn never to do, he dropped his rifle and ran to get Desrosiers.

In a moment, it was over. With the decision of a man already condemned to die, Rolf swooped out into the open amid a rain of eager bullets, tucked his arms under Desrosiers' shoulders, and whisked him behind the opposite side of the barricade. No one saw; no one noticed. And Rolf was grateful nobody thought to scream at him for risking another life when lives were already scarce. A twinge of soreness ran through his arm—was Desrosiers, thin as a stick, really so heavy? A trickle of blood pooled in his palm—Desrosiers'? When he tried blindly to pick up a rifle someone had dropped—whose was it?—he couldn't seem to close his fingers around the trigger.

Desrosiers was conscious, it seemed, because his hands clawed Rolf's jacket. "What are you doing?" he screamed hoarsely, his mouth full of dust. "Point that gun at the enemy, not at me!"

"Don't hold a gun if you don't know how," growled a voice in Rolf's opposite ear. Auclair seemed to possess a supernatural ability to teleport wherever his orders were most needed. "Get inside and get that arm looked at. We'll talk about what you did later."

Rolf hadn't even noticed where he had pointed the rifle. He had pointed it at someone because that, he thought, is what rifles are for. But who was it? Across the barricade? Behind? At Desrosiers?

What was he doing, and who was he shooting?

Something rough smacked his face, and he found himself staring into Auclair's watering eyes. "Get inside. Take Desrosiers with you. Don't make me repeat myself."

"So, you ran out and got him." The nurse pulled the bandage tighter, and Rolf flinched. "That was courageous." Her tone conveyed the equivalent emotion as commenting on the weather.

"It's his first time seeing combat, too!" Desrosiers gushed, trying to sit up but unable to pull his chest close enough to his elevated leg. "He should get a medal for conspicuous bravery! Not that I'm anyone important, of course. It's too bad he didn't save a general."

"Do you really think I'd be a pacifist if this were my first time in combat?" Rolf interrupted sourly. "That's enough, nurse. I need to write."

She clicked her tongue and gave his bandages a final tug. "You won't be writing until your arm heals."

"It's just a graze."

"Your nerves are shot."

"I'm not nervous."

"Not *those* nerves. Your fingers are twitching."

Rolf clenched his fist. "I'm fine." He glanced at Desrosiers, propped against a pile of green wool coats with his leg elevated on what might have once been a small trash can. "Will he be all right?"

"I'm great!" Desrosiers assured him with a salute. "I'm alive! What more could I ask for? And now, I have an excellent story to tell my grandchildren and an even more excellent chance of getting an extended leave at a field hospital behind the frontlines." He winked at the nurse. "You'll see to that, won't you?"

She pretended not to hear him, staring hard at a tray of half-empty bottles—iodine, alcohol, something else Rolf couldn't read—and twisting a small glass syringe between her fingers. Perhaps, he thought, she didn't want to make promises she couldn't keep.

"Good luck." Rolf's smile was one-sided. "Maybe I'll get my newspaper to mention your name. I'll tell them about the young French soldier so brave, he ran out in front of heavy fire without even stopping to think."

He did not wait to hear Desrosiers' outburst of gratitude. There was a shadow pacing up and down outside the window, and Rolf knew he could not start writing his report until he vindicated himself.

Auclair turned toward him the moment he appeared in the doorway. The major's face was streaked with grime, through which Rolf could barely make out his expression; and his uniform was torn around his chest, grazed by a bullet.

"What newspaper do you write for?" he asked abruptly.

"*La Liberté*," Rolf answered, frowning. "This is stated in my paperwork."

"I thought you wrote for a British paper."

"Yes. It's called *Liberty* in English."

"I've never heard of it."

"You are not English. And I am not a well-known journalist."

"Yet your paper thinks highly enough of you to send you all the way out across the Channel, when they could copy reports from journalists at more . . . " Auclair paused. "Affluent papers."

A quick grin crossed Rolf's lips. "Are you calling me a nobody?"

"I am saying that your history is as watertight as a sieve." Auclair did not return his smile. "I don't know what you're doing here, Mr. Writer, but I hope you do it and get out as soon as possible."

"I have nothing to hide. You can read my dispatches if that would convince you."

"I don't doubt I can." Auclair nodded. "You can go."

"Aren't you going to ask me about earlier? You said I made a mistake with my weapon, where I pointed it. But I swear, I had no idea where I was pointing it. It's my first time in combat—real combat, that is."

"Well, you're a journalist. Maybe you just don't know how to use a gun. It wouldn't be so strange, would it?" The downward curve of Auclair's lips suggested that he did, in fact, find it strange. "Get some sleep."

Rolf nodded. But the moment Auclair vanished around the corner of the munitions truck, he sat down on the steps of the apartment building—or was it a barracks now?—and fished two pens and a notebook from his pocket. One pen he tucked behind his ear. Clenching the other in his left hand, he wrote one laborious letter, then another. His hands shook, and the ink pooled and splotched. But the mess hardly mattered. Rolf's letters were best when they were illegible.

When he had struggled through a few lines, he stood up, stretched, and went back into the "hospital" (the bottom floor of the building across from the "barracks"). Though the sun was half-set outside and the buildings' shadows covered the street, he had to wait for his vision to adjust to the dim, murky interior. He wished he had trouble hearing instead of seeing. Whispered conversations, hurried orders, screams, curses—these were commonplace. The calm patients were worse. They had nothing to lose, and they knew it. They, too, were already condemned.

Rolf picked his way through rows and cots—some empty, some occupied, others messy but abandoned. He knew what these meant.

Some of the patients met his curious gaze; others ignored him; others were asleep or unconscious. He scanned each face carefully, passing from row to row until he came to the last bed of the last row, crammed into the back corner of the room.

"Wake up," he said in Italian.

There was a rustle from under the bedsheets, and a pair of terrified brown eyes peeked out.

"Will you live?" Rolf asked him.

Slow nod.

"You owe me."

Another nod.

"If you value your life—no, if you value mine, since we are countrymen—don't you dare say you know me. You almost gave me away yesterday. If I hadn't put that cloth across your mouth, you would have let the secret slip."

"I will not." The deserter's hands trembled as they clenched the blanket. "You have my word."

"Why do you look so frightened?" Rolf's smile was stretched. "I've done nothing but help."

The man remained silent.

"What's your name? I'm afraid I don't remember you."

Long pause, and then: "Andrea . . . sir. You were my instruc—"

"Well, Andrea, if you're worried about your conscience—since, after all, you are on *their* side now—be at ease. This is the letter I received a month ago." Rolf pulled a crumpled wad of paper from his pocket and handed it to Andrea. "You can see it's genuine. I have perhaps a week left."

Andrea read it silently, and Rolf twitched it from his fingers the moment he looked up.

"God bless you," the deserter muttered.

"Be grateful He has not, or else you'd have a dilemma on your hands." Rolf replaced the letter in his pocket and offered a mock salute. "Get well soon, Private—or whatever rank you are now. I won't come see you again."

Chapter 4

It is a peculiarity of some farsighted people that the closer you put a book to their face, the less they can make out the words. We are guilty of such hyperopia here at the front. For we are at the front—indeed, we are the front, in many ways—but we have less knowledge of what is happening than the generals back in England. They can tell you about the thousands of men killed during this war, but we can only tell you that Jones had his leg blown off one day and Jacques showed signs of tuberculosis the next and that they were carted off to the hospital where they may have died—or perhaps lived—but no one informed us.

—December 17, 1940

If anyone at the Censorship Bureau had thought to toss Rolf's letter into an oven (which, of course, nobody did), the heat would have revealed a different message.

I was afraid to do the math before; but time is running short, so I have finally worked it out. They told me a little over a month when they sent me here. Thirty-three days until they give the French my name and send me to my death. I wanted to see Christmas once more, but they have made sure I can't even beg for something so

simple. On December 24 it seems, they will trade me; and I am sure
to be shot immediately. My life for five French prisoners. Perhaps I
should feel flattered that they think I am worth so much. I do not.
I would rather be worth nothing at all if it meant that I could see
the Colosseum once more.

The letters were smeared, the words hastily scribbled, misshapen,
and ugly—much like how he felt when he wrote them. Gaps here and
there where letters were missing or illegibly distorted, an absent "e"
on one line and an uncrossed "t" on the next, betrayed that he had
not only failed to proofread but had also paid only minimal attention
to what he was writing. He knew it made no difference what he said,
much less how he said it. The "friends" he was writing to would know,
by the time it reached them, what had happened. They wouldn't care
much, maybe not even enough to bother revealing the invisible ink,
because what was he to them? Merely someone from whom they
got meager information about meager things, someone who wrote
at length about how terribly this war bored him and how much he
wished he had expressed his gratitude for the things he took for
granted at home. He was a telegraph, transmitting information day-in
and day-out without having anything to say itself. When a telegraph
breaks, it is replaced.

But who exactly were his friends? He had shot at his own troops,
picked up a rifle and defended the men he was supposed to betray. He
told himself it was for his "cover," that he couldn't do anything else
and remain unsuspected; but he knew how his mind worked. He'd
done what he did because he wanted to do it. That was why he did
everything. Why, then, was this what he wanted?

Perhaps, he had failed his mission the moment he condescended to note, in his very first letter, that war created misery. This observation probably succumbed to the censor's blot because nobody was supposed to be miserable, especially not during a war that freed them by eliminating their desire to be free. He should never have said that, should never have acknowledged that he was capable both of feeling despair and of creating it. It had been the first step toward admitting he had done both, and it had led him to feeling—

Sorry?

Regretful?

Ashamed.

He caught a glimpse of himself in a shard of Desrosiers' shaving mirror. His was not a pleasant face. His false naivete clung to him like the ink clung to his fingers; and his own expression made him nauseous because it was so wrong, so misplaced, so disassociated from reality. There was no coming home for people like him, no rebirth, restart, re-anything. If they were sending him "home" in exchange for some hapless prisoners of war, who was he to complain? Perhaps, he'd be useful for the first time in his life, getting those poor devils sent back to their families.

For once, his endless well of excuses had dried up. Lacking those made him feel curiously lonely.

Fabric swished behind him, and he started up from his chair. But it was only Desrosiers, come to ask for a sheet of paper.

"To write a letter to my mother," he confessed shyly.

"Here you go." Rolf steadied his hands enough to tear a sheet from his notebook. "Where's your mother from?"

"A little village in the south. You won't have heard of—"

"Roussillon?"

"How did you—?"

"It is my business to know these sorts of things. Now, go write your letter," Rolf told him, shooing him out of the room and nodding and smiling and clenching his fists. "And say something to her about me, will you? Say you think I'm deranged, or my pencil scratching annoys you. Anything helps, if only someone remembers something."

He pulled the door shut behind Desrosiers, and then he curled himself up on his cot under his tattered blanket, tucked his wounded arm to his chest, and went to sleep.

Chapter 5

I want to give a girl a flower. It's the kind of thing you think you can do anytime you please. Walk down the streets of Rome (am I allowed to say this since everyone will know tomorrow?) with a rose in your hand, and you will see a score of women who deserve it, and whose week would be substantially improved if you gave it. But you never do, and the reason is that you could do it anytime. You put it off until one day, you find that you have lost your chance, and then—not until then—you miss it.

—December 23, 1940

He thanked the nurse who had bandaged his arm. She took his thanks as a matter of course. After all, what wounded soldier with a bullet in his shoulder who felt he'd been torn back from the brink of death wouldn't bless God for her capable hands? But Rolf had never been under the illusion that he was dying nor that he needed her help for a procedure he could easily have carried out himself. He was grateful—not for her assistance, but for her humanity. And he couldn't tell her that, so he simply gave her a tip of his cap and a dry smile.

He gave Desrosiers a notebook, clean and pristine from cover to cover. He might as well have given him a sheaf of money, the way the boy's eyes glowed.

"For me?" Desrosiers asked not once, not twice, but three times, as though Rolf's generosity were supernatural. "I'll use it well," he promised, stowing it under his pack where no one could steal his treasure. "You're wonderful, Allard! A real *camarade de régiment!*" He smacked Rolf's shoulder. "Let us stay together until this war is over, and then I'll buy you a drink at the *Place de la Revolution.*"

Make right the things you have made wrong. Undo what you have done. Don't ask for forgiveness—they will never grant it—but keep it to yourself and let them think forever that you are better than you are. It will hurt you worse than it will them.

He left his rifle and ammunition in Auclair's room. That way, when they came to arrest him, he would be unarmed. And Auclair needed the ammunition. He was a soldier, not a sneak. He did his fighting fairly. So, Rolf also left his personal arms—an Italian-made pistol and a box of high-quality rounds, the kind he had long ago spent freely as air—in a neat pile under Auclair's bed. He'd see it when he washed the blanket, which he did methodically once per week and which he'd do again after the . . .

Saying the word directly gave him a bad taste in his mouth.

Execution, you coward. Say it.

"I'm not a coward."

Say it.

"I'm not afraid to die."

"Death" is what happens to soldiers. "Execution" is what happens to rats.

"I'm not a rat."

You're worse. You're a lying rat.

Rolf's hands clenched around his blanket. "I did what they told me to do."

Could you say that to Major Auclair's face?

"I did it when my country was still a good country."

The "country" has never been good or bad. It's only you. You, the representative. You, the people. You who make it into a cohesive whole. It's you who has gone bad.

"Shut up!" Rolf screamed, squeezing his hands over his ears until his head ached and his knuckles bent backward. "You don't know anything about me. You don't know what I've done—not why, not for whom, nothing. You know nothing—not about me, not them, not why I'm here, not what they've done. Take your disgust and your hate and your reproaches and burn them in a ditch. A mine on the beach, an explosion, and it's over. That's all you're worth. That's all anyone's worth, and I'm no different than anyone else. Why does it matter what I did when the worst offenders will never face justice?"

They will.

"No one has seen what they have done."

The world is soaked in blood. The rivers stream it. The heavens rain it. Everyone has seen.

"And what does 'everyone' do but bayonet and shoot and blow up and make more of the same destruction?"

There's a day for war. There's never a day for slaughter.

He woke up with sweat pooling at the base of his spine, sitting straight up in his bed, cheeks wet, hands shaking, and chest so tight he could barely breathe.

"I did everything right at the end." Tears streamed through his fingers and splattered on the blanket. "I undid everything I did as best I could. I know I was wrong to fight for them, and I've done my best to change. There's nothing more I can do. Second chances are a child's fiction."

The voice that spoke in his dream—the one that was half imagination and half audible—whose was it? It sounded like Major Auclair. But it sounded equally like Desrosiers. And it had a feminine quality that reminded him of the nurse, but it was harder, too—like the deserter who had desperately tried not to show he was afraid. It was all of them at once, screaming like seagulls around a dead fish.

He swung his legs off the bed and onto the cold dirt floor, savoring the way it froze his aching muscles. He pulled on his boots and coat and padded out into the darkness. Except it wasn't dark, not in the usual sense. The war did not take breaks to let soldiers sleep. The sky burned orange as tiny suns rose and set, floating up, falling down, synchronizing with a distant explosion—and, sometimes, if it was close enough, someone's strained voice yelling orders.

These lights lit his path along the piles of disintegrated rubble crowding the streets, through which he had to pick his way as carefully as though they were living people, for they were just as much in his way. He got a rock in his shoe, but he didn't stop to shake it out. Doing so would mean being spotted from a window. And being spotted from a window would mean a death that came too suddenly and conveniently to be deserved.

He tripped over a broken stone, scraping his palms and leaving streaks of blood on the rocks. One particularly bright orange flash cracked the sky. The ground shook. Dust scratched Rolf's face. Pebbles rained on his head. He looked up, and there in front of him was a steeple. Tall and dark, backlit by flame, it towered above him and poured debris into the street and onto his back. He scrambled to his feet and instinctively dove out of the way of something. What was it? Looking back from the shelter of an imploded porch, he saw it was an iron bar that had dug itself so deeply into the ground that it stood upright, next to where he had been kneeling.

Don't kneel in front of the church, sinner that you are, or Heaven itself will cleanse you from the earth. A grim and lovely irony.

On top of the steeple was a cross. One side was broken and dangled off at an odd angle. Rolf had the impression that it, too, might fall on him if he so much as coughed. It swung loose in the wind, and he thought he could hear it creaking.

"That could've been you," he said aloud to himself, eyes fixed on the broken cross. "If you had listened, maybe you wouldn't be afraid of that thing."

Listened? To what? Himself? To the voice in his head, whatever—*whoever*—that was?

"It could still be you," he whispered. He did not believe that, but it sounded nice.

He took one step, then another, then a third; and unexpectedly, he was standing on the steps of the church. Blazing heat scorched his face. His skin was parched, and his hair crackled. Wind swirled around him under his coat and shoes until it might lift him and hurl him into the furnace that burned inside that church that had melted the cross on the steeple. It ached, shivered, gnawed. Yet he had to get closer. Why? Who knew? Who asked? He reached a hand to open the door. The wood scalded his fingers; and without thinking, he screamed.

Why was he here? What had he done to deserve this? The answer was clearer than the pain in his hands. He had been a boy when he had joined the Italian army. His training had begun with two years of rough-and-tumble education in a special division, where he had been kept cloistered as a monk to keep him clean of the "corrupting" influence of the outside. Two weeks of questioning came after, where he was asked about his birth; his parents; his home life; everyone he had ever known, read about, seen, heard of, or talked about; and some things he did not even know he knew.

Once they had heard everything about him—when they were certain of who he was and who they could make him—only then did they let him leave, and only then did he see the world for the first time through the eyes of a man. What a strange and uninteresting sight it was. They had told him that he was supposed to be the Roman Odysseus—cross the seas and win fame that reached the skies and come back and get the girl. But he was a boy who had become a man too quickly, who had a little gift for writing that was abused until it became scratches on paper that nobody read, invisible ink, and the lowest kind of treachery.

He staggered back, tripping on the hot stone steps and barely regaining his balance by seizing a piece of fiery wood. He screamed again, frustrated, and all he got for an answer was the harsh scraping and swinging of the broken metal cross high above his head. Then it fell. It landed inches from him, so close he could feel the ground shake under his feet and the added heat of the simmering metal blast his skin under his coat.

Behind him was the church. Before him was the cross. To either side were sunken ruins of burned buildings. North, south, east, west—there was no escape for a godless man.

"Please!" he shouted, shielding his face with his arm. "I understand. I'm done! It's over! Do with me whatever you please; kill me if you must. But please, if you are the kind of God Who deserves a cathedral like this—if You are really greater than this lovely place—please, if You can, forgive me."

The fire tickled his shoes. He kicked an ashen log; and it disappeared in sparks, dousing the fire that was closest but leaving the tide of flame behind it raging high. He considered vaulting over the cross, but that would only land him in a sea of molten . . . something. He couldn't tell what it had once been. Maybe a piano. He thought he smelled veneer.

"*Vous!*"

He must have been dreaming.

"*Tenez-le!*"

He'd gone crazy from the smoke. He heard a voice—that much was certain. But who would be calling to him from within the inferno?

"*Dépêchez-vous!*"

His voice wanted to stay buried in his throat, but he managed a hoarse, "Auclair?"

"Grab the rod, you—" The major added a fantastically untranslatable curse. "Get moving, or we'll both be *brulés vifs!*"

Much to Rolf's astonishment, the long metal bar of the cross heaved itself upward and hovered above his head. He seized it with both hands. It seemed cool to the touch, and he grabbed it tighter. It dragged him, then lifted him over the flames. As he rose, he saw Auclair hauling down the other end of the bar, which was balanced precariously on the dented roof of what had once been a military vehicle. A lever. A brilliant testament to Auclair's inventiveness and to whatever power had made the bar land the way it did.

He landed on his feet, and he tried to dust the ash off his uniform pants; but his hands filled with raging pain as the raw, burned skin scraped the canvas. He wondered how he had ever been able to grab the bar and hold on so tightly.

"Why are you here?" he asked, trying to focus his eyes on his rescuer's grimy face.

"I saw you leave. I came after you." Auclair grabbed his arm, which Rolf could barely feel, and dragged him to shelter behind a house that had not yet caught fire.

"Why?" Rolf asked when they could hear each other. "Why follow me?"

"I was going to shoot you."

"Why?"

"Don't you know I know?"

"Know what?"

Auclair's laughter had a sharp edge. "A British journalist arrives with a bag full of nothing but paper and chocolate, has an Italian accent, calls himself by a German name, speaks French fluently, and says he's a pacifist? A novelist couldn't make it up. Only a government could flaunt a story that ridiculous. You're Swiss-Italian, I've no doubt. And those are just about the only two countries you omitted to mention in your papers."

"They said it's what you'd want to hear." Rolf was too exhausted to attempt a denial. "They said you're short of chocolate. Said you feel sympathy for the Italians. Said you can't bring yourselves to hate the French and German half-breeds. Said you wish you could be pacifists. They said you wouldn't notice if I said it confidently."

"I don't care if you're German or Italian or English or Chinese." Auclair had his pistol out, cocking it, raising it, pointing it at Rolf. "You're a dirty traitor. They'd give me a medal. If I let you walk away, I'll be the one committing treason."

"Then shoot."

The church door caught fire, roaring into flames that sent a hot wind gusting past their hiding spot.

"You fought with us."

"I suppose."

"You saved Desrosiers."

"Yes."

"Why?"

"He needed saving."

"He's your enemy."

"It was the first thing I thought to do. You saw that I pointed my rifle at him afterward."

"It was a reflex? That's all? You really saved him just so you could shoot him?"

"Yes."

"Were you going to pull the trigger?"

"Yes." Rolf's cheeks flushed hot.

"You're lying."

"I am not."

"You are." Rolf understood what he meant: *you'd better be.*

"I am . . ."

And then, gazing absently over Auclair's shoulder, he saw the girl.

She was a long-haired little girl, her white skin streaked with black ash, face glowing in the fire, seven years old, if he was generous. Her frilly white dress was as incongruous as a smear of chalk on a blackboard. She couldn't be there—shouldn't be there—clutching a book, crying, face streaked with ash and white-powdered ceiling paint.

She was too small, too vulnerable. Wide-eyed with terror, she stared at him and sobbed bitterly.

He held out his hands. She stayed where she was, tears streaming, shaking her head.

"Come here," he ordered.

Still, she did not move.

"Please, little girl—"

It started as a whistle. It grew to a shriek, and then it overpowered everything. Rolf couldn't hear it anymore because it became a blanket covering the earth and dousing the fire and flattening the houses with the sheer power of its volume. He ran before he knew what he was running from. He had the girl in his arms, and he pinned her to the ground under him—that was the key point; that was what he had to do. He held her tight and forced her head under his chest, and then he closed his eyes and prayed and maybe screamed, too, though he couldn't hear himself any more than he could hear the rocket.

Something hit him in the back. Or maybe "hit" was too strong. This touch was softer, like a tap—a very gentle tap.

For a moment, it hurt but not very badly.

And then he found he didn't need to breathe. He couldn't breathe, even if he'd wanted to.

And then he fell asleep.

Chapter 6

"Rolf Allard, twenty years of age, killed by a falling beam."

Such a memo would be shorter than a court-martial. The papers would get shipped off to somebody higher-ranking than Auclair, and that would be the last anyone heard of Rolf Allard. No one besides Auclair and perhaps a few obscure generals would have to know he was a spy, so he could do himself a favor by dying quietly.

But there was a problem, and that problem was sitting across the room staring at Auclair with sea-blue eyes and lips that trembled like a leaf in the wind and a dress that was soaked in the back with someone else's blood.

"Little girl," said Auclair, squirming under her inflexible gaze, "Why don't you go home?"

Her house was standing, and her parents were alive. The only reason she'd been out on the street during the bombing was because she'd somehow gotten lost on the way to the shelter.

She didn't answer his question, only kept looking, boring holes through his head with her pale eyes.

"Will he live?" she asked at last.

"Turn around," Auclair ordered.

She obeyed, and he wet his handkerchief in his canteen and tried to scrub the blood off her dress. But he might as well have tried to mop a puddle with a broom. No amount of scrubbing would get the fabric clean, and it was so thin that it would rip if he kept scraping it with his rough handkerchief.

He unbuttoned his uniform jacket and handed it to her. Her shoulder dipped under its weight, but she held it sturdily aloft.

"Take the outer part of your dress off," he said, pointing to a little closet in the corner, "and fold it up. Don't look at it. Put this jacket on and bring me your dress."

She toddled off, hands balled tightly around her skirt, and reappeared a few moments later with Auclair's coat dragging the floor behind her. Her hands had vanished, swallowed in the long woolen sleeves; and the collar was so high that she had to hold her chin up to see over it. She handed him her dress, rolled up tightly, and he put it on the chair beside him.

"Now go home, little girl."

"I'm Francine."

"Go home, Francine."

"Will he live?"

"Yes."

She shook her head. "Will he live?"

"Little girl—Francine—why are you staying where you don't belong?"

"Don't I belong here?"

"The hospital is for people who were wounded in the war. People who are wounded in war are soldiers. You are a girl. It's you who . . . " He sighed, looking down at his boots and noticing, inanely, that there was an irritatingly symmetrical x-shaped scratch on one toe. He'd have to fix that later. "It's you who makes us think we're fighting on the right side. You have to stay behind because we can't lose you, too."

"Will he live?"

Auclair chewed his lip. Finally, he said, "I don't think so."

The blue eyes filled with tears.

"What do you care?" he asked roughly, turning away. "You'll forget him in a year or two when this war is over."

She dropped into a heap at his feet, wailing and shrieking. A nurse glared at Auclair—*get your brat under control before we kick you out*—and before he knew exactly what he was doing, he found himself picking her up and holding her in a bundle of scratchy green wool in his lap.

"I'm sorry I said that." Why was he apologizing to a child? "I'm sorry you've seen this. I'm sorry we're fighting here on your doorstep. I'm sorry . . . "

"Will he live?"

She seemed to think he had a choice. Of course, he didn't. Even if Rolf survived his wound, which he wouldn't, he'd be court-martialed as a spy. And even if he survived that, which he wouldn't, there was still this ghastly war that would probably plant him, Auclair, Francine, and all of them in the ground sooner or later.But he found himself saying, "I think he will." He half-believed himself.

Somebody screamed, a terrified, achingly lonely scream. Auclair cupped his hands over Francine's ears. She must have heard it; but instead of pulling away, she snuggled into his coat and hid her face in his sleeve.

"You are a nice man," she announced, wrapping her hot fingers around his thumb.

A peculiar label, Auclair reflected, *when I hold another man's life in my hands. Is it fair?*

A thought scrabbled in the back of his mind, a thought he didn't like but couldn't quite stifle. *There is always a choice. Rolf will only die if you let him.* Ridiculous. Illogical.

Yet compelling.

Edging through his hazy mind was the book by which everything in his life was ordered down to the way he tied his shoes—the *Armed Forces Manual*. There was something in the book—a mention of a special case or something. He couldn't remember the details.

"Nurse!" he barked, startling the child in his lap. "Do you have a copy of the manual?"

Of course, they did not, properly speaking, but the nurse indicated that a commander had recently been killed; and his personal items were still on the floor near his cot. Auclair placed Francine on the chair next to him, promising he'd be back in a moment, and rifled through the dead commander's luggage. Sure enough, there it was, thick and obtrusive and impractically heavy. Only a commander, Auclair reflected ruefully, would bother carrying so much dead weight. But Auclair was grateful he had.

He sat down beside Francine, but she had already fallen asleep; so he spread the heavy manual across his knees and absently flipped through the thin pages. This is what you do if one of your soldiers disrespects you. This is the minimum quality of your ammunition (and it was mostly lies, in his experience). This is how we treat prisoners-of-war.

This is how we treat spies.

We kill them, of course.

But then, there was *la Règle d'amnistie.* The Amnesty Rule. *Because there is always an exception for mercy.*

He found the right page among the thousands of wrong ones and read the words aloud—curiously, slowly, as though he'd never seen them before.

"Article twelve, section fifteen, point four: if an enemy soldier performs faithful service to the French National Army, and if such soldier be judged by at least three soldiers in good standing who know him well and have witnessed his service to be a friend, and if such soldier renounce his citizenship in the country whose army he serves and publicly pronounces himself a defector, he shall be given asylum in France and held innocent before the law of treasonous acts. He shall not be permitted to enlist, and he shall be held under arrest for the duration of the war, after which he shall be released upon good behavior and given the opportunity to become a citizen of France."

It was all so simple—such an egregious loophole, there for any man with evil intentions to take advantage of—and why? Why keep that rule when it could be so deadly dangerous?

A smile pinched Auclair's thin lips.

War has taken enough of our humanity. But it could never take it all.

"Merry Christmas," a voice growled, distant and fuzzy. "Wake up and enjoy it. You're not going to see another."

"Christmas?" he mumbled, trying to open his eyes. But they were so heavy. A sliver of light poked through his lids, and he shut them again.

Something slapped his face. "Sit up straight when I'm talking to you."

Rolf attempted to obey, purely out of instinct, but his muscles refused to respond.

"I received a letter yesterday," Auclair continued. The harsh crackle of paper unfolding grated on Rolf's ears. "From none other than General Juin. He says there is to be a prisoner exchange, and as of yesterday afternoon, you are mine to do with as I please. He says you are a spy for the Italian army, and he says I should attempt to extract information from you." The paper was refolded, and Rolf heard it rustle against the cloth of Auclair's uniform. "What do you think?"

"I'll tell you whatever you want to know."

"Why would I believe you?"

"I don't know. I wouldn't if I were you."

"Do you understand how miserable I can make you? I can torture you. No one will ever have to know what happened if I tell my men you are a spy and you tried to ruin everything they are dying for. They'll enjoy watching you suffer. And if that's what it takes to keep them safe, then so be it."

"I suppose you think I deserve it. I don't disagree." Rolf settled back into the pillows—real pillows, he noticed, not a pile of uniform coats. "I have known since before I came here that you would receive that letter on December 24. I knew you would kill me. I have known all along."

In the distance, Rolf fancied he could hear somebody laughing—a girl's voice, if he had to guess. But it might have been nothing more than the squeaking wheels of the nurse's medical cart.

"You've known for a month?" Auclair said at last. "Is that why you were so careless about keeping your cover?"

"Why bother to be a liar when it does no good?"

"And you want to give me information . . . why? To get back at your handlers?"

"No." Rolf managed to sit up about halfway before he flinched and dropped back to the pillows. "I was wrong. I saw the cruel things my country has done, yet I refused to take responsibility as a citizen. I stood by and watched and participated, saying I was unwilling but doing nothing to change. I should have died when I was trapped in the fire—that would have been a fair punishment—yet I didn't. For some reason, I was given a second chance. Or a reprieve. Why, I don't know."

"God bless you," Auclair mumbled.

"He has." Rolf's lips crinkled into a small smile. "I have already asked God for forgiveness. He has given it. I don't expect you to do the same, which is why I am offering you all the information I have as an apology."

"Give me the short version."

"The Italians are preparing to invade. They are sending soldiers to train with the Germans; and when those men return to Italy, they will be sent across the border near Monaco. The goal is to pinch the French army between the Germans, the Italians, the sea, and the Spanish border."

Auclair retrieved the letter from his pocket and scribbled a hasty note. "Can they succeed?"

"Maybe. But they are distracted by internal struggles. You could take advantage of this if you play your cards right."

"Do you know more?"

"Yes. I'll write it all down in as much detail as I can."

Auclair tapped his pencil against his leg.

"Desrosiers and that deserter—Andrew? Andrea?—have both agreed to testify on your behalf," he said suddenly. "If I also put in a good word, you wouldn't be executed. You would be under guard, of course—more or less a prisoner of war. But you'd be set free once the war ends."

"Why would you let me live?"

"You saved Desrosiers."

"So?"

"You saved that girl."

"I did?" His eyes flickered. "Thank God."

"You've done things you couldn't do if you were loyal to the enemy."

"Maybe it was on instinct."

"You said that before, but I don't believe you. You're not an automaton. You think on your feet. You're a man." Auclair stood up. "It's your choice. Forswear your allegiance to the Italians, or be executed by the French. I have no personal interest in your decision. You seemed like someone who was worth a chance; but if you disagree, then so be it."

More laughter, tinny and high-pitched and irreverently happy. Was it that child with the long hair and the tearful eyes? Rolf's mouth was dry, and he had to lick his lips before he could speak.

"Before God and man, I forswear my allegiance to the Italian army. I recognize the wrong we have done, and I will do anything to help make it right."

"Fine." Auclair nodded. "Now that we've settled that, perhaps you should look outside."

"How . . ." Rolf began, but Auclair had already seized the bar at the top of his cot and begun rolling him toward the window.

"The State has no money for fireworks this year," he said, "but we don't lack explosives." There was a hint of humor in his voice. "It's a joy to waste them on something like this."

Against the black night sky, a streak of orange fire shot straight up like an exploding star, like a guide to light the path. At the peak of its arc, it burst into a shower of sparks that rained down over the skyline in dangerous, glittering beauty. It was aimed at nothing and had hit or hurt no one. It was just an exuberant expression of joy in life and, Rolf thought, gratitude that weapons of death could also be instruments of peace.

"Welcome to France, Rolf Allard," Auclair murmured. "Merry Christmas."

CHAPTER 8

Who else could have brought me back from death when my warrant was, quite literally, signed, sealed, and delivered? If Auclair had not found me at the church, if he had not seen me save the little girl—Francine—if he had not been given the courage (and, perhaps, corresponding foolishness) to believe in me, I would be dead, forever to remain the spy, never to become the man.

Christmas, they say, is the season for miracles. For the French army, it was merely an additional season of pain, during which we— they—hoped for a miracle that seemed like it would never come. As individuals, however, no one gave up hope. And for me, the miracle that took place thousands of years ago—which gave us a reason to celebrate wildly and burn explosives without targets and forget, for one night, how miserable we are—came fully before my eyes. The burning cross trapped me in the fire and forced me to decide: Purify my sins before the cross and beg for the forgiveness I did not deserve, or burn eternally, branded a coward and a liar. I did not deserve that opportunity to change my path. God provided it.

The war dragged on long after. The devastation might never reach its end. But we, the people, live; we continue to fight. We have not given up hope that things will change. All the little tasks that are forgotten about during a war—the woman who sells flowers, the man who writes serial novels in the newspaper, the children who serve food in restaurants—these are all of monumental importance now because they show that we have, again, become humans who place extraordinary value on tiny slivers of beauty. As a country, as a world, we have been given a second chance. To seize it with both hands, as I seized the cross Auclair extended to me over the flames—this is our mission, beyond a battle or a war, for which we have been given life.

—December 2, 1949

RESCUE: A CHRISTMAS STORY

ALLEN STEADHAM

Chapter 1

WALLY CARSON REACHED INTO HIS jeans pocket and pulled out a quarter.

"Do I clean the apartment or go into work on my day off?" he wondered aloud.

He flicked the coin into the air, caught it on the way down, and slapped it onto the top of his hand.

"Tails," he told himself. "Fine. I'll go and see if they need help at the store."

He pulled on his thick gray jacket as he caught a quick view of his mother's picture on top of his dresser. He tried to ignore his messy bed, the overflowing laundry hamper, and the sports magazines littering the floor.

I'll get to it, he thought.

He stopped, bowed his head, and closed his eyes to pray. *Lord, I'm still praying, like Mom taught me. Please help me make some kind of sense out of my life. Every day flows into the next, and I don't know what to do.*

Wally slumped his shoulders and let out a heavy breath. *I'm only twenty. I never had big plans . . . and maybe I should have. I don't know. I was happy enough with Mom. Lord, I really do need Your help. In Jesus' name, I pray. Amen.*

A few moments later, he exited his apartment, locking it on the way out. He passed one of his neighbors and her young son on the sidewalk between buildings.

"Afternoon, Mrs. Cooper," he said, giving her a quick nod as he continued walking.

"Afternoon, Wally," she replied, nodding back. Then she added, "Merry Christmas!"

He turned his head toward her and half-heartedly smiled. "Merry Christmas!"

As he continued toward the parking lot, he shivered against the cold and biting wind, but the blue skies and bright sun lifted his mood some. Grabbing his keys from his front right pocket, he unlocked his used blue Ford Ranger truck and climbed inside.

Traffic was especially light today, even for a small town. As Wally drove down Main Street, he noticed the Christmas decorations on the light poles lining either side of the street. He looked up and saw green garlands wrapped in white lights stretching across overhead, along with electronic and paper banners wishing the townspeople "Merry Christmas" and "Happy Holidays." He remembered that many had left to visit family in the bigger cities, returning after Christmas or the New Year.

"The mayor really did go all out this year," he said with a smile. Then he returned his attention to the road in front of him.

He turned right at the next intersection and pulled into the Ryker's Groceries parking lot. He got a good spot near the entrance of the large, cranberry red, wooden building. The signs in the windows and entrance advertised the latest specials on produce and meats. Next to the store's parking lot was a clothing store. Across the intersection was a tire shop and the city fire department.

Returning his attention to the grocery store, he noticed that there were hardly any customers going in or coming out.

"Did I make the trip for nothing?" Wally huffed. "Oh well, I'm already here."

Walking inside, he immediately observed that many of the shelves were half-bare, especially beneath signs offering 30 to 40 percent off those items. There was an elderly couple near the freezer section and a young woman with a basket near the bread aisle.

"Wally?" a man's voice asked to his left. It was the manager and owner, Thomas Ryker. "What are you doing here? It's your day off."

Wally turned to face the burly, salt-and-pepper-haired man with glasses and a scruffy beard. "I thought I'd come in and see if you needed any help."

The older man smiled and considered his words. "I don't think we'll have many more customers. I'll probably be closing early, maybe in a couple of hours."

Wally sighed. "I understand."

"You can help me close down the store, though. Go ahead and tidy up the shelves, then sweep the floor and clean up in the back."

Wally's spirits immediately lifted at the request. He didn't want to go back home for nothing. "Yes, sir! I'll get right on that. Thank you, Mr. Ryker!"

Aleta Jiménez was lighting the last of the Christmas candles in the duplex she shared with her boyfriend, Roman Finch. She had spent the last week decorating the living room mostly by herself, though Roman had gotten the Christmas tree and strung up the lights on the front of their side of the duplex.

She wanted to surprise Roman with a cozy setting when he returned from a long day as a roofer. He made a good living with his skills, but it was often thankless and physically punishing work.

Aleta had adorned the Christmas tree with a variety of metallic ornaments in shades of red, green, gold, and silver. She had placed several wrapped gifts beneath the tree on its sparkling green tree skirt. With the natural late afternoon sunlight combining with the candles' illumination, the room had a tantalizing air that sent a tingle down her spine and made her grin in anticipation.

Roman has his faults, but he tries so hard to do right by me, she thought. *I want this Christmas to be perfect for both of us!*

Roman was twenty-five and she nineteen. She thought he was handsome with his piercing brown eyes; angular face; shoulder-length, scruffy, black hair; and long bangs. A few inches taller than she and muscular, he could be charming, tenderly praising her beauty as he declared his love.

As she walked toward the kitchen, she looked at the dark walnut cabinets and matching dining room table he had crafted for her just months earlier. He'd made a project of it after she had made one remark about wanting better ones. He had an artist's talent and a working man's strength and tenacity that she admired.

She allowed her imagination to run free for a moment: She pictured Roman walking through the front door. He would look tired, as always, but he'd have a smile for her. And as she ran to greet him, he would pull a small box from his pocket and go down on one knee before her.

"Aleta, will you marry me?" he would say.

She would clasp her hands together and nearly swoon before answering.

"Yes! Of course, I'll marry you, Roman!"

He would then stand up, place the ring on her finger, and share a long, passionate kiss with her.

Roman had been sitting in his car alongside the curb facing the duplex for the last ten minutes. He'd already finished four beers and thrown the empty cans in the back seat. He was halfway through the fifth, working up the resolve to go inside and face his girlfriend. He looked over to the passenger seat, where a paper bag sat, filled with one bottle of champagne and two bottles of wine.

He sighed. "She wanted this year to be special."

Finishing his beer in attempt to gain "liquid courage," he tossed that can in the back. As he stepped out of the car with the paper bag in one arm, he shoved the door closed and stood up straight, breathing in the cold air. Then he ambled forward up the driveway, unlocked the door, and went inside.

He put the bag on the floor and took in the sight of all the living room's Christmas decorations.

"Wow, that's nice," he said softly. "She made it really nice."

He stumbled forward, losing his balance. He grabbed onto the Christmas tree, which was never going to support him, and made himself quickly shift positions so he could lean against the nearest wall instead of falling.

"Whew!" he exclaimed. "That was close."

Still holding the tree in his arms at a fifty-degree angle, he looked up at the golden star atop it.

"You get me, don't ya?" he said. "I used to be the nice guy. Nice Guy Roman . . . who helped people, did favors an' stuff. But . . . people use the nice guy . . . and expect so much." Without realizing it, Roman began to drift forward with the tree. "And when things go wrong, who's the first one they blame? Me!"

Gravity did the rest.

Aleta's daydream was interrupted by something crashing onto the floor in the living room. Startled, she leaned around the corner from the kitchen. Roman was home early from work. He had laid a paper bag on the floor and fallen into the Christmas tree, knocking it to the ground and smashing several of the ornaments in the process.

At first, she put her hand to her mouth and gasped. She was very worried about him. But he pushed himself up off the floor and looked at her with a crooked, intoxicated smile.

"Sorry 'bout that," he said, laughing. "I kinda lost my balance."

"Babe, it's only four," Aleta said, shocked but holding back her ire. "Why are you home early? And why are you drunk?"

Roman pushed himself to a seated position on the floor, putting his hands on his legs to keep him semi-upright.

"I got into an argument with the boss, and he fired me," he replied. "But he did gimme my last check, so I got some stuff for us to party. Christmas, y'know?"

Aleta crossed her arms and scowled at him.

Roman's expression collapsed, and he sighed as he maintained eye contact with her. "I'm sorry."

Wally made sure to do a good job over the next two hours to justify his employer's trust in him. He was in the middle of sweeping the floor when he realized the irony of his circumstances and chuckled to himself.

I gave myself the choice of cleaning my apartment or cleaning my workplace, he thought. *Either way, I ended up cleaning. At least, I'm getting paid for this.*

Ten minutes later, he had completed the sweeping and walked to the front of the store to see his boss.

"Great job, Wally," Ryker said, handing him two large paper bags filled with groceries.

"What's this, sir?"

Wally took a look into the bags in his arms. He was amazed to see there were fresh vegetables, canned yams, cranberry sauce, butter, a box of stuffing, and a fully sliced ham from the deli.

"Make yourself a nice dinner tomorrow. You've had a hard time of late," Ryker added. "My wife and I wanted you to have a good Christmas."

"Thank you, Mr. Ryker," Wally said, deeply touched by the gesture. He blinked away an unexpected tear. "Please thank your wife for me. I hope you and your family have a merry Christmas!" Mr. Ryker thanked Wally and patted him on the back as he walked out the entrance.

Wally secured the bags in the back of the cab under the seat. He started to imagine the meal he would make.

Aleta still wasn't happy with Roman. Sitting in the passenger seat of his red Chevy Camaro, all she could do was stare at him in disapproval.

"What?" he asked, taking notice of her simmering gaze. "I said I was sorry about earlier! I'm even taking you to a fancy restaurant to make it up to you."

"A meal at a fancy restaurant isn't going to make you more sober. I should be the one driving, you know," she replied spitefully. "It also won't get you another job."

"I'll get another job," he boasted. "And soon!"

He blazed past a stop sign and screeched around a corner, almost hitting a parked car.

"I don't think you're okay to drive, Roman!"

"I slept off most of the booze. I'm fine," he insisted.

She took a calming breath and tried to sound pleasant. "Pull over and let me drive, okay?"

He turned his head suddenly and looked at her with anger. "I *told* you I'm fine!"

Returning his view forward, he sped up, almost outrunning the headlights. It filled Aleta with new anxiety. She grabbed his arm and squeezed.

"Roman, please pull over and let me drive!" she exclaimed. "You're scaring me!"

He ripped his arm away, gripping the steering wheel with his other hand.

"Are you crazy?" he shouted. "You coulda caused me to have a wreck!"

"That does it! Pull over and let me out—NOW!" she shouted back. "I hate it when you're like this!"

She saw a familiar fury erupt in Roman's eyes as he squeezed his right hand into a fist and started slowly lifting it up.

It was then that an old, icy fear clawed at Aleta's heart.

Wally was less than a mile from the grocery store when the gas light flickered to life on his dashboard. He confirmed that the gasoline indicator was all the way on "E." And it was getting dark outside.

"Shoot! Are there any gas stations still open near here?"

Just then, he remembered the Husk gas station at Liberty and Third Street. He knew the truck was riding on fumes at this point. And he wouldn't make it back to his apartment on that. Moving slowly along the deserted downtown road, he tried to let the vehicle coast as much as possible, conserving his remaining fuel.

As he turned left onto Liberty, he spotted the station.

"Yes! The lights are on—they're open!" he proclaimed. Then he looked at the gas prices on the marquee. "Unleaded is a little steep, but I'll take it."

He coasted the truck to a stop next to the nearest pump, yanked out the keys, and ran inside the station. The dark-skinned man with thinning white hair gave him a kind smile.

"Five more minutes and I'd have closed up and left, son," he told Wally. "What can I get ya?"

"Thirty dollars on Pump Two, sir," Wally replied, handing over a twenty and a ten-dollar bill.

The station attendant pressed a few buttons on the register and nodded. "Okay. You're good to go on Pump Two."

"Thanks!" Wally said as he went back outside. "Um, merry Christmas!"

"Merry Christmas!" he heard the other man respond cheerily.

Wally had never been so relieved to pump gasoline into his truck. Thirty dollars wouldn't completely fill it, but it was enough to last a week or more. The pump automatically cut off as it reached its limit.

Right now, Wally just wanted to hurry home and stream a movie or binge-watch a television show.

Aleta thought she heard Roman's voice, but everything was a numb haze. That is, until the side of her face throbbed with near-blinding pain.

The pulsing fire sensation morphed into a deep soreness and brought her to full consciousness. And the memory of what had just happened propelled her into action. Not caring about their speed or location, Aleta unbuckled her seatbelt, shoved the passenger door open, and leaped out of the car. Adrenaline shielded her from the sting of impact on the two-lane road and motivated her to get up and break into a full run away from Roman.

She heard the tires screech as they brought the car to a halt, the sound of the door opening, and Roman calling after her. Her panic pushed her forward.

Wally only had a split-second to wrench his steering wheel to the right. His peripheral vision detected motion, a dark-haired young woman running into the poorly lit road directly in front of him. If he made the wrong choice, he'd hit her, hurting or killing her. So, he swerved away. That decision had immediate consequences, as his truck missed the woman by inches but sideswiped a parked delivery van for the already closed Rose's Roses. Ricocheting back to the left, the pickup's momentum forced it to roll onto its side and skid to a halt. The instant his vehicle hit the pavement, Wally's head smacked the driver's side window.

Everything seemed to slow down, and he was enveloped in conflicting sensations of warmth and pain. It was difficult to focus his vision. Then he heard a thumping sound several times in a row. When he opened his eyes, he beheld the silhouette of a woman in front of him. She was banging her fist against the windshield.

"Hey! Can you hear me?" she shouted, her voice muffled by the glass. "Can you get out of the truck?"

Wally wanted to reply that he could, but that would've been a lie. He couldn't make his body do what he wanted yet. His limbs trembled at his sluggish efforts. When he tried to speak, he coughed. And something smelled like smoke.

Aleta felt her adrenaline spike and had to clamp down a growing sense of apprehension. Only seconds ago, she had been running for her life and hadn't seen the approaching truck. She'd thought she would die, yet the driver missed her.

All of the businesses had shut down early, and there were only a few cars on the street. She had no one to assist her. It was dark, and the streetlights had just turned on automatically. The truck's driver was barely moving.

He's hurt! I don't think he can even move, she thought.

She turned her head to look at the hood of the truck. A small stream of smoke was escaping in odorous wisps. She didn't know if it was from an actual fire or just a damaged electrical system. She was too short to reach the upturned passenger door. So, she went to the back of the truck and looked for anything to help free the man. Near the driver's side of the tailgate, she espied a gray toolkit and a long tire iron. Without hesitation, she grabbed the very solid-looking tool and ran back to the windshield.

She wondered if she really had to smash the glass and drag the injured man out somehow. But no one else was around; she'd lost her cell phone on the way here, and she couldn't call for help. The truck's hood was becoming warm, and the amount of smoke was increasing.

"I'm sorry about this!" Aleta exclaimed as she swung the tire iron at the windshield.

It bounced off, only scratching the center of the glass. The second time, she put all her strength into the effort and shattered the windshield. It sprayed across the seat and the driver.

She reached inside the cab and unfastened his seatbelt. The driver was looking at her a bit more wide-eyed, his attention captured by the breaking of the glass. That encouraged Aleta, but he still appeared groggy.

"I need to get you out of your truck," she said slowly, emphasizing each word to him. "It's not safe. Can you move?"

He nodded. "Y-yeah, I think so."

Aleta left the tire iron on the hood and wiped as much of the shards off the dashboard as she could. "Crawl through the opening I made," she urged. "I'll help you, okay?"

Without a word, the young man did as instructed, inching forward on all fours toward the hood. Once he had crawled most of the way out, she grabbed his hands and pulled him toward her. Putting an arm around him, she tried to guide him toward solid ground. Once on the pavement, she grabbed the tire iron from the truck's hood and let the man lean on her until they made it across the street. The wind was picking up, causing the nearby trees to sway. It was getting colder, too.

Aleta was grateful that this man was tall and slender. But she was concerned about his head wound, a jagged and bleeding cut above his left ear.

He looked very familiar to her.

We're close in age, she thought. *Did we go to the same school?* When he groaned in pain, she snapped out of her introspection.

"I need to get you to a doctor," she suggested. "Do you have a cell phone?"

"Truck . . . it's in the truck," he replied woozily.

Aleta turned her head and saw flames starting to spit from underneath the hood with puffs of black smoke. Going back for his phone wasn't an option. She knew it was only a matter of time before the truck was engulfed in flames. It could even explode.

Aleta led the man to the next block as quickly as she could before they stopped and sat down on a bus bench. She heard a car door slam nearby and let her hopes rise at the possibility of rescue.

"Aleta! There you are! What are you doing? Who is that guy?"

Those hopes were immediately dashed, and she felt a cold wave of dread descend over her. That voice belonged to Roman.

Of course, he tracked me down, she thought bitterly. *He always does.*

She looked at the injured stranger, then to Roman.

This guy needs help and Roman has a car, she thought. *But would Roman do it?*

"Hey, it took me forever to find you! I just wanted to make sure you were okay," Roman interjected, sounding irritated. His eyes were laser-focused on her, and his arms and hands were open in a questioning manner. "You jumped out of the car while it was moving. That wasn't safe!"

She fumed. "And why did I do that, huh?" she bellowed, pointing at her swollen left eyelid. She could only imagine how bad it looked.

He stepped forward undeterred. "I'm sorry about that. Just come with me, and I'll make it up to you."

Aleta attempted to calm herself. She pointed at the injured man next to her. "This guy was in an accident. Can you—"

Roman's full attention was only on her. And he looked like he was running out of patience. "Let's *go,* Aleta! Just you!"

There! That proves it, she thought.

Aleta looked down at the tire iron in her left hand, suddenly glad she'd decided to bring it with them. She turned her attention back to Roman and projected months of pent-up frustration at him.

"No more making up! You have a problem that I can't fix. Find someone else! I'm done," Aleta declared.

Roman took a few more steps toward her. She noted the fresh stench of alcohol from where she was.

He's still drunk, too. This is bad.

She stood up and let the blond-haired man slump onto the back of the bench. When she took a step toward Roman, she was ready to attack him with the tire iron, brandishing it like a sword close to her chest. She vanquished all fear and let herself channel rage.

"Last chance, Roman!" she shouted.

"You're bluffing," he replied dismissively. "You'd never hit anyone with a thing like that!"

She tightened her hands around the tire iron and smiled menacingly. "Do you wanna find out how wrong you are?"

They exchanged a long, unblinking stare for almost thirty seconds. Then she saw a hint of what looked like fear in his eyes. His lips twisted into an ugly frown, and his pride reasserted itself through his petulant gaze. He actually looked offended.

"You know what? Have it your way," he answered with a sigh. "We're done."

She was tempted to say something incendiary but figured that was a bad idea.

"By the way, it's miles to the hospital from here; and I have your phone. Good luck finding someone to help you," he taunted as he walked across the street to his Camaro. He got inside, started the engine, and looked at her a final time.

"Merry Christmas," he sneered.

Chapter 2

Wally's head still hurt and was damp. He touched near the cut. The sting made him recoil his hand, and his fingertips were now coated in blood. The pain dispelled his grogginess, at least temporarily, and returned his attention to his surroundings. It sounded like a man and woman arguing.

As his vision cleared, he started making out details around him. He knew he was still near downtown. About twenty feet away from him, he saw a black-haired man of average height with a muscular build. Facing him was a plump woman with wavy dark brown hair. From what Wally had heard, they had been in a relationship. But now, she was defending herself from the man with what looked like a lug wrench.

As the other man finally drove out of sight, the woman let the lug wrench fall to the ground. Her eyes were wide; and to Wally, she appeared dazed or maybe in shock. Slowly, she turned to look at Wally.

He didn't know who she was, but he was almost certain she had saved his life. He made himself stand up, even though his balance was wobbly.

"Hey, are you okay?" Wally asked innocently.

"Oh! I'm sorry you had to see that, especially tonight," she replied, clearly unsettled. "Um, I'm okay. I've . . . just been through a lot with that guy. We, um, we should keep moving. We need to get you seen by a doctor."

With the mention of a doctor, he focused in on her injured eye and immediately sympathized. It was a darkening red and purple blemish. *She needs to be seen, too,* he considered. The thought of anyone hurting her upset him.

He was still struggling to keep his mind focused.

"I'm Wally," he said with a strained, breathy voice. "You got me out of the truck, right? Thanks."

"You're welcome. I'm Aleta. Are you gonna be okay? You hit your head pretty hard."

"I'll probably need some stitches. But that guy was right about the hospital being far."

❄ ❄ ❄

Aleta barely heard the last thing he said.

His name is Wally? I remember a Wally . . . from high school.

She gazed at his face for a few more seconds. Then she looked down, searching her memories.

One image stood out: blond hair in the wind, a boy breaking into a run after making a solid hit to the ball. She could see his excited dash to first base and a daring slide to second.

"Wally Carson?" she blurted, surprising them both.

"Yeah, that's my name," he replied. "You know me?"

An embarrassing thought froze her in place, leaving her mouth agape for a moment. Then she recovered.

"We . . . both went to River Valley High," she told him in a matter-of-fact tone.

You were on the baseball team, and I had the biggest crush on you for six months during my junior year. My girlfriends and I went to every practice and most of the games to watch you guys.

"Oh," he said. "Sorry I didn't recognize you."

"It's okay. Don't worry about it."

She looked skyward for a moment, noticing the clouds and feel of the air. She looked down at what she was wearing—a black jacket, dark purple sweater, blue jeans, and tennis shoes. And then she peered at Wally, who had on a gray jacket, red t-shirt, jeans, and brown boots. At the moment, their present circumstances were far more pressing than the past.

"We're gonna need a miracle," she said under her breath.

"What's that?"

"It's getting colder, and I think we're in for sleet or snow soon," Aleta said with some concern. "We better start for the hospital now. Can you keep walking on your own, or do you need to lean on me some more?"

"I'll be okay for a while," he answered.

Wally only made it about a block and a half before he felt dizzy and stumbled. Aleta quickly caught him.

"What's wrong?" she asked.

"I feel lightheaded; it's throwing off my balance," Wally replied. "And I feel sleepy."

That alarmed Aleta. She was no doctor, but she had enough sense to see the problem.

"You need to stay awake. We won't— You can't sleep right now, okay? Talk to me, Wally; tell me about yourself. Do you live here, or were you just passing through?"

"I grew up here," Wally offered, blinking a few times to maintain focus. "My mom moved here when she was pregnant with me—you know, to get a fresh start."

Aleta nodded. "How far does she live from where we are now?"

Wally lowered his gaze somberly. "She died two months ago from cancer," he said softly.

Aleta's jaw dropped. "I am so sorry!"

She saw Wally point a trembling finger to their left. "I live in an apartment on the west end," he said. "On Third Street. Been there about two years."

Aleta's eyes flashed with recognition. "I used to live over there when I was growing up," she said warmly.

"Small world, huh?" he replied with a hint of a smile.

They both looked at each other and then straight ahead as they started walking again.

"Small town," they both said in mutual amusement.

They continued along the sidewalk in silence for a minute.

"It's always been enough for me," Wally said. His lips smiled; but when she caught a glimpse of his eyes, they had a weariness to them. His voice was straining from his efforts to keep walking, but it was also tinged with grief. "Living here, just me and Mom. Even when I got a job and moved into my own apartment, I still stopped by or called. Mom and I could talk about anything at any time."

Aleta smiled as she sympathized with him. "She was your best friend."

"Yeah. And now, she's gone."

She wasn't sure how to respond to that. She just did her best to keep physically supporting him.

They limped along another couple of blocks before Wally had to stop again. This time, they both sat down on a curb and leaned against each other for warmth. Their breathing made puffs of condensation in the freezing air.

"You managing?" Aleta asked.

"Somehow," Wally acknowledged. "I think the cold is helping me not feel as much pain."

"At least, it's good for something."

Wally closed his eyes and started losing consciousness. Aleta grabbed him by the shoulders and shook him back awake.

"Hey, stay with me! Okay, Wally?"

He took in a deep breath of the chilly air and opened his eyes again.

"Tell . . . tell me about you, Aleta," he said weakly.

She tried to keep from frowning, but she didn't like talking about herself.

"What's to tell? You know I grew up here, too. I had to leave home . . . a couple of years ago. I stayed with some friends, started working, and was planning to get my GED and go to college. Then I met Roman."

She could tell Wally was trying hard to listen to her, but it was taking a serious effort. She squeezed his shoulders with just enough force to get his attention. "Roman was already working, really talented, and good friends with his boss. I fell in love with him. I . . . thought we had a future . . . until I broke up with him tonight."

Wally breathed in deeply, looking over at her. "I noticed you said you had to leave home. Can I ask why?"

Aleta gripped her shins and looked away.

"If you don't wanna talk about it, it's okay," Wally added sympathetically.

"My dad was like Roman—violent toward me and my mom," she admitted. "Mom stays with him, but I had to get away."

She turned her head to see Wally's reaction. His eyes were compassionate and kind, though he had grown paler and had to squint from his pain now and then.

"Aleta, you've been such a help to me tonight, a real lifesaver," he told her. "I want to help you. And I guess I have to do it now . . . You know, make it count."

"What do you mean?" she asked. *I don't want to hurt his feelings, but he can't even stand up*, she thought. *How can he help me?*

Aleta noticed a few flurries drifting to the ground. She looked up and saw more, the light of the streetlamps illuminating them as they fell. She couldn't help but notice how pretty they looked.

At the same time, they represented the very problem they were facing. Her fingertips, nose, and lips were freezing and starting to go numb. She was sure Wally was just as cold.

"I shouldn't go any further, the way I'm feeling. But I want you to go," he said. He looked around for a moment until his eyes settled on one area nearby. "If you can get me to that area between buildings across the street, I'll be okay. You can get to safety and send help for me."

Her eyes widened. "No! It'll take too long for me to get to the hospital! And it's freezing now." Aleta just stared at him a moment. Then she made up her mind. "I won't leave you."

She helped him stand once more. "We'll both go over there, but I'm not leaving you." He nodded, and they made their way to the space between the local barber shop and an insurance office. After sitting back down, they looked at each other for a moment. The snow flurries were beginning to accumulate in their hair and on their jackets.

Wally's eyes fluttered. He was falling asleep again, and that worried Aleta.

How can I keep him awake? she wondered frantically. *I can't just keep shaking him; he has a head injury.* Only one idea came to mind.

"Do you still play baseball?" she asked, nudging him as lightly as she could.

"W-what?" he replied. His eyes barely opened, but she had his attention.

"Baseball," she repeated. "Do you still play?"

He struggled to sit up some, so she helped him do that. He cleared his throat, which ejected a big white breath cloud. Seeing him starting to shiver, she pulled him closer and wrapped her arms around him.

"H-h-how did you know I play b-baseball?" he asked, his teeth chattering.

Aleta leaned her head against his shoulder and sighed. "Because I used to watch you at practice."

"You d-did? Why?"

She laughed in spite of herself. "Why? What girl *didn't* want to watch Wally Carson, the Home Run King of the River Valley Tigers?"

"Who called me that?"

Looking up at the falling snow, she smiled in reminiscence. "I may have been the first to call you that . . . but it caught on," she told him. "A lot of us called you that."

"It n-never got back to me." He sounded a little dejected.

"That's okay. It would've just gone to your head," she joked.

"So . . . you were my fan . . . back then?"

She turned her head and made eye contact with him to see if he was serious. And he was. She could tell he had no idea about her feelings.

"I was *in love* with you, Wally," she told him. "You're tall, handsome, a talented baseball player. And you were safe."

He leaned forward some and put his arms around her, but his grip was very weak. "Safe?"

"You were a real-life fantasy," she continued hesitantly, looking away. Her cheeks felt flushed. "I could watch you with my girlfriends and enjoy your accomplishments from the stands. But I didn't have to risk being rejected by you."

His eyes widened. "What? Why w-would I reject you?"

"I've always been a big girl," she said shyly, looking down. "Big girls don't get the athletes. So, after a while, I found another fantasy boy for a while. And then later, I found Roman." She sighed.

"Hey," he said. His voice was almost as weak as his grip, but she heard a new seriousness in it. She met his gaze again. "You'd have gotten . . . *this* athlete."

She briefly shook the mounting snowflakes from her hair, and her mouth fell open. "What did you say?"

"I . . . didn't really date in high school, Aleta. But if I'd known you liked me, I would have gotten to know you. Mom taught me that people come in all shapes and sizes, and that's okay. She was kinda big, too . . . till she got sick."

His words cut through her, even though he'd meant no harm. As she lowered her head again, she felt a tear roll down her cheek and half-expected it to freeze midway. She was terribly cold now, even with Wally's form blocking some of the wind.

I could have been with Wally, if only I'd had the courage, she thought bitterly. *I didn't have to be with Roman at all.*

He seemed to pick up on her souring mood. With some effort, he placed his hand on her shoulder.

"Y-you know, if we survive this, I'd . . . um . . . " He stopped himself, looking down.

"If we survive this, you'd what? Tell me," she insisted.

"I . . . like you, Aleta." That surprised her. "I know things are really bad now . . . but if we make it past tonight, would you consider going out with me?" he answered. She could tell he was trying to smile, despite his shivering and pain.

She briefly smiled also, then re-focused on their situation. "Our surviving might be . . . optimistic at best."

He nodded, shivering. "I know."

She pulled her hands in front of her and rubbed them together. Then she sank them into her coat pockets. Though all kinds of thoughts ran through her head, one kept repeating; she didn't know why, but it gave her hope. Finally, she had to say it, no matter how it sounded. "Even so . . . listen, if we survive this, I'll marry you!"

Wally stared at her in amazement for several seconds. "Was . . .was that a proposal, Aleta? You serious?"

She wondered if he was right. Had she just offered to spend her life with her high school crush? Then she thought about everything that had occurred this evening and the past couple of years. In a surreal way, it made a kind of sense.

After a moment, Aleta shrugged. "Why not? We're probably going to die, so let's be honest. I already know you would treat me better than Roman. I'm willing to give it a shot."

Wally smiled and forced his quivering hands together. He held them below his chin and closed his eyes.

"What are you d-doing?" Aleta asked.

"Praying," he replied.

"What? Why?"

"Because . . . I've got something to live for now," he exclaimed. "I want a miracle!"

She smiled and closed her eyes. "If you think it's a good idea, I guess I'll try, too."

A short time later, someone laid a heavy, insulated blanket on Aleta. She heard the same person lay another blanket on Wally next to her. Two hands gently shook her shoulders to wake her up. Then that person did the same for Wally. Aleta opened her eyes first. Her feet, legs, and fingertips were numb; and her hair was frosty and stiff in places with frozen precipitation. She made herself focus on this man. She had never seen him before. He looked to be maybe in his thirties and tan-skinned, wearing light-colored clothing. He had dark hair, a trim beard, and a kind face. He put something in her hands. It was a cell phone.

"Miss, use this to call 9-1-1. Stay on the line with them until they arrive," he told her in a reassuring tenor voice. "You two will be all right. I have to go."

"Wait! What? How?" Aleta sputtered. "Could you help us get to a hospital?"

When she looked around to locate the man who had saved her and Wally, she couldn't see anyone within a one-block radius. It was as if he'd completely vanished.

She noticed that the snow had lightly coated the street and the tops of the vehicles, trees, and light posts. It had gotten even colder, and the breeze had picked up some. She heard a soft groan next to her. *Wally!* In a panic, she turned toward him, ignoring how cold and numb her legs felt. His eyes were closed, and he wasn't moving; but his moans showed he was alive and in pain. She grabbed his arms and shook him in desperation.

"Wally, c-come on, wake up!" she urged. She saw his eyes flutter. "I have a phone. I can get us help now! I need you to stay awake just a little longer, okay?"

His eyes opened more fully, and he focused on her face. He was so pale. "Okay . . . okay, Aleta."

Only then did Aleta do as the stranger had instructed and called emergency services. After the operator answered, she kept talking to him until the ambulance arrived. When she ended the call, she took a close look at the phone.

It was hers.

Chapter 3

ALETA WAS SO WORRIED, RIDING in the ambulance with Wally and the two Emergency Medical Technicians (EMTs). Wally's breathing was very shallow. The EMT had strapped him onto some kind of board and secured Wally's head into what the EMT called a cervical collar. He had also placed an oxygen mask on his face to help with his breathing. Wally looked so pale and helpless, frighteningly still under the blanket the EMT had used to cover him.

Aleta wasn't in much better shape. Now that the immediate threat of freezing to death was gone, she could focus on other things—like how much her head hurt and the deep achiness in her ankles and legs. And she was still cold, so very cold. She was wrapped in the heavy blanket the stranger had given her, but the iciness seemed to permeate her entire body. Even so, she was more worried about Wally than herself.

"Please . . . W-Wally!" Aleta exclaimed through chattering teeth. "You've got to make it!"

"My teammate is doing all he can for your friend, and we'll be to the hospital in about five minutes," the other EMT replied calmly. She was a middle-aged woman with graying brown hair pulled back into a short ponytail. "I'm more concerned about you. Take some slow, deep breaths."

Aleta tried to take the breaths, but she started to cough on the second one. It took a few seconds to stop coughing.

"You've been through a lot tonight," the EMT said sympathetically. "You're half-frozen and in shock."

Aleta pulled the blanket tighter, but it didn't make her feel any warmer.

The EMT handed her an ice pack. "You've got a pretty bad shiner. Hold this against it," the EMT added, pointing at her own left eye. "And I noticed other bruising on your neck and chest." Then she nodded her head toward Wally. "Did he do that to you?"

Aleta shook her head in horror. "No! This happened just before we met!" She hesitated, softening and lowering her voice. "It was my ex-boyfriend who hit me."

The EMT nodded in understanding.

"Wally and I . . . We thought we were going to die," Aleta said hoarsely. Then she looked over at Wally and smiled. "But he prayed for a miracle . . . I did, too . . . And we got one."

That caught the EMT's attention. She looked at Aleta curiously. "What kind of miracle?"

"We didn't have phones," Aleta answered. "My ex had mine, and his was in the crashed truck."

The EMT narrowed her eyes in confusion. "But you called 9-1-1 to tell them where you were. Whose phone did you use?"

Aleta grinned. "That's the miracle!" She reached past the blanket into her jacket and pulled out her cell phone, explaining what had happened to her.

The EMT looked skeptical but smiled, anyway. "Good Samaritan, huh? Well, you reached us just in time. Another hour and your friend might not have made it. Neither of you would have survived the night in this weather."

"A Good Samaritan miracle," Aleta said under her breath, smiling as she surrendered to fatigue and unconsciousness.

Roman was startled by the WHOOP! WHOOP! noise that sounded behind his car. But when the red and blue lights began to strobe, followed by the police flashing their brights, he knew he was in trouble. He cursed in resignation and slowly pulled over to the side of the highway before easing to a stop.

The police cruiser stopped a full car-length behind him and let its lights continue flashing. A minute later, a tall and muscular male officer in a dark gray uniform began to stride toward him with a bright flashlight in hand. Roman had left his window half-open and kept his hands on the steering wheel, making no provocative moves. The officer leaned forward to make eye contact with him.

"Did you have a little too much holiday cheer tonight, sir?" the dusky-haired officer began. "You were weaving and going about twenty miles under the speed limit."

"I had a couple of beers," Roman lied, trying to be pleasant. "And I'm almost home, officer. Sorry to trouble you."

The officer smiled. "It's no trouble, sir. May I see your driver's license and proof of insurance?"

Roman carefully retrieved his wallet from his back pocket and his insurance card from the glove compartment. He nervously handed them to the officer, who inspected them in the flashlight's illumination.

"Mr. Finch, this insurance expired two months ago," he said calmly. "Do you have a more up-to-date copy of your proof of insurance?"

Roman sighed and sunk into his seat. "No, sir."

The officer nodded. "I see. Would you be willing to submit to a breathalyzer test?"

"Sure. Why not?"

"Thank you," the officer said. "I'm going to get the breathalyzer and check a couple of things. Please stay here."

Roman felt like a trapped animal. He put his hands over his eyes and let his fingers part as they slid down his face. As the policeman returned, Roman started to break into a cold sweat in dreaded anticipation.

The officer had him breathe normally into the device. It didn't take long for the results.

"Mr. Finch, please step out of the car," he told Roman. "And put your hands behind your back."

Roman complied, crestfallen at his misfortune. "Is it *that* bad?"

The officer put handcuffs on him. "The legal alcohol limit in Texas is .08. Yours was .16. You also were driving without auto insurance, and there was an arrest warrant issued for you tonight over assault charges."

Roman sighed more deeply and shook his head in denial. The officer began to lead him toward the police car. "Mr. Finch, you have the right to remain silent . . . "

Aleta awoke feeling sluggish and dry-mouthed. She was briefly confused by her surroundings, a spacious room with the only illumination coming from the brightly lit hallway outside a slightly opened door. She was grateful for the warm, thick blankets covering her.

That's right, she thought, relieved. *We were on the way to the hospital.*

Now in one of the hospital beds, she lifted her arm and noted the I.V. line that was giving her fluids. Looking over at the window, she could see it was still dark outside and that snow continued falling gently.

How could something so beautiful nearly kill us? she wondered.

Aleta reached down and found the nurse call button and pushed it.

Seconds later, a man answered.

"Yes? How can I help you?" "Can you send my nurse in . . . please?"

"All right."

"Thank you."

A couple of minutes later, a woman with dirty blond hair entered the room, leaving the door halfway open. She appeared to be a few years older than Aleta, tall with a sturdy build. She smiled, but her eyes showed concern.

"Hi, I'm Greta, your nurse for tonight," she said in a smooth alto voice. "Did you need something?"

"I had some questions," Aleta said, sounding raspy. "And I'm really thirsty."

Greta poured her a cup of ice water and handed it to her. She took several big sips before handing it back to the nurse, who put it on the nightstand next to her bed.

"I thought they were gonna treat me in the emergency room and let me go," Aleta wondered aloud.

The nurse shook her head. "No, unfortunately you had a moderate case of hypothermia and dehydration, along with your other cuts and bruises, so Dr. Kensington had you admitted for observation and recuperation."

Suddenly, Aleta looked around the room and then back at the nurse. "Do you know how my friend is? We were on the ambulance together," Aleta inquired with some urgency. "His name is Wally Carson."

Greta smiled reassuringly. "He's in the room next to yours. I can't give out specific medical information, but he's doing better."

Aleta closed her eyes and sighed gratefully. "Thank You, God."

Greta left the room, and Aleta laid back down. Her thoughts remained on Wally.

Wally Carson . . . my high school crush, she pondered. *He hasn't changed. He's still a good guy. He wrecked his truck and got injured to protect me. When he told me to leave him and go find help, he was willing to sacrifice his life so I could get to safety.*

She sighed and turned her head on her pillow to face to the window.

All my life, I've either put up with abuse or run away from it. But I can tell, Wally isn't that way! He's not selfish like Roman . . . or my dad. Based on his actions, I feel like he'd put me first.

She turned her gaze to the ceiling.

I said I'd marry him. Do I already trust him that much?

She closed her eyes, and her thoughts drifted back. The day before, she had imagined Roman proposing to her and swooning at the idea.

I had high hopes for me and Roman. I loved the idea of being in love with him. She felt herself frown. *And I know Roman cares—well, cared—for me. Maybe between the security his job provided and the way he treated me when he was sober . . . maybe I thought that was enough. I believed I could make the difference; I could make him happy, and then he wouldn't hurt me.*

She put her left hand to her bruised eye and sighed.

But I can't change him. Only he can do that. And I won't wait around for him to change.

When she thought about Wally again, her heart swelled in anticipation.

Wally, you've got to be okay. I want to be with you.

Just after eight o'clock the next morning, Dr. Mark Kensington entered Aleta's room. She was awake. Greta had checked her vitals before her shift ended. The African-American doctor was tall with an average build. Perhaps in his late thirties, he had kind brown eyes, a wide smile, and a bald pate.

"Merry Christmas!" he said brightly in a deep tenor voice. "I'm Dr. Kensington. How are you feeling this morning?"

"Merry Christmas! I feel a lot better," she replied.

It was the truth, but her concern was more for Wally.

The doctor nodded. "Your blood pressure and heart rate are certainly better. Your bruising should heal in a week or two. Do you wanna get out of here today?"

Aleta nodded enthusiastically. "Yes! I'd love that."

So I can check on Wally, she thought. *He was hurt worse than me. How much longer will he have to stay in the hospital?*

Dr. Kensington flashed a new smile. "Consider it done—my Christmas gift to you."

"Thank you, Doctor!"

"Go ahead and have some breakfast, and I'll get your paperwork started," he added. "We'll have you out of here in an hour or so."

"Thanks again, Doctor. And merry Christmas!"

"You're welcome," he replied, nodding and waving as he left the room. "Enjoy the rest of the holiday!"

Wally had never had such a rough night. He barely remembered being put on a board and strapped into a neck brace for the ambulance ride to the hospital. He had never felt so persistently cold. It was a struggle, since he wanted to sleep so badly. However, just like when Aleta warned him not to sleep, he sensed the same importance in the EMT's tone of voice and fought to obey. The result was jarring blurs of light, sound, and sometimes motion. Finally, someone injected pain medication into his I.V. line and granted him the peace of a deep and dreamless sleep.

It was late morning before he regained a semblance of awareness. *At least, I'm not cold anymore,* he thought. It felt like he was under some heavy blankets. He took a few deep breaths and released them through his mouth.

Wally didn't expect Aleta to be the first person he saw when he opened his eyes. But she was sitting at his bedside smiling at him with misty eyes.

Several seconds passed. At first, she seemed content that he was doing better. But there was also a growing affection between them. He could tell by the warmth in her eyes.

"Aleta?" he asked weakly.

She didn't respond at first, looking a bit uncertain. She wiped a tear from her right eye.

"Um, welcome back."

"Thanks." *What is this feeling between us?* he wondered.

"We . . . we survived Christmas Eve," she continued, still sounding hesitant. "We got to the hospital in time."

"I guess so, huh?"

When he moved his head to get a better view of Aleta, his neck resisted him with its stiffness. And though some kind of medication had significantly reduced his head pain, it wasn't entirely gone. He leaned back against the pillow and closed his eyes to endure these sensations. Just then, he felt Aleta quickly take his hand in hers.

"Hey, don't overdo it," she urged. "You're still recovering."

He took a few moments to absorb her words and let his body settle down again. He realized she hadn't let go of his hand. And he was okay with that. He opened his eyes again. She was in last night's clothes. It looked like she'd brushed her hair.

"How about you, 'Leta? You okay?"

She laughed, not commenting on his new affectation for her. "Me? I'm fine. They released me two hours ago."

"What's . . . so funny?"

She closed her eyes and chuckled briefly. "You were in a crash and nearly froze to death. You're still in a hospital bed . . . but you're worried about me?"

"Yes." He lifted his other hand and reached for her face. She leaned forward and let him brush his fingers along her left cheek. "You were hurt, too."

She shrugged to one side. "They treated me; I'll be okay. On the other hand, you had a concussion and needed ten stitches. Plus, you had hypothermia on top of that."

He blinked a couple of times in confusion. "How'd you find that out?"

She leaned forward again and grinned knowingly. "I told the nurse I'm your fiancée and bugged him to tell me!"

Wally looked at her with some concern. "Are you sure?" She squeezed his hand a bit tighter. "Hold me to it."

"What?"

She tenderly took his hand in both of hers and gazed at him softly. "I meant what I said. We were . . . reunited through crazy circumstances; and we nearly died, but I saw you—the real you—last night. And you saw me."

Wally was speechless. What she said was true.

"I realized some things while we were out there in the cold," she continued. "I wished I'd have had more confidence back in high school. I should have talked to you and told you my feelings." She chuckled. "Who knows? Maybe we'd have been a couple all this time—maybe married. I don't know. Most of all, I wish I could have been there for you when your mom was sick."

He was deeply moved. "I would have liked that. It was a bad time . . . for Mom and me." He wiped a tear from his eye. "I think Mom would've liked you. And she'd have been happy to know I had someone supporting me."

Aleta was still holding his hand, but she leaned her head on the bedrail. "I have so many regrets about my choices over the last couple of years. I want to do things differently now."

He squeezed her hand. "You can. God gave us both a second chance last night."

She kissed his hand, then returned her gaze to him.

"You're right," she replied, grinning nervously. "Wally Carson, I love you. I've loved you since I first saw you."

He stared at her in awe. Her words and actions made him feel lighter than the medication, practically giddy.

"Aleta, you're a good woman," he said humbly. "You saved my life twice, got me out of my truck, made your ex-boyfriend leave, and stayed by my side till help arrived. You risked death when you could have saved yourself."

He decided to kiss her hand in return. "And bruise aside, you're very pretty."

She blushed and smiled. "You think I'm pretty?"

"Yeah," he said with a smile. "And . . . you've won my heart, Aleta. Will you marry me?"

Aleta had never felt like this before. As she looked over at Wally, she was genuinely happy that the color had returned to his handsome face, and there was a new sparkle in his boyish green eyes. She felt a warmth being close to him and holding his hand. She wanted to protect him.

"Yes, I *definitely* will marry you!" she declared proudly. At that moment, she let go of all caution. "Can we—can we get married today?"

Wally's eyes widened, but he never lost his smile. "You want to get married on Christmas?"

She lowered her head and let go of his hand to grip the bed's side rail.

"I haven't put faith in much before," she said quietly. "But I can't ignore what happened, either. We prayed, and we got an answer. A man came out of nowhere and gave me my phone to call for help. Maybe that wasn't a man. Maybe it was an angel!"

Wally seemed to consider that, then nodded. "Maybe it was."

She nodded, too. Then she put her hand on his arm and looked at him once more.

"So, I was thinking if God went to so much trouble for us to meet in this crazy way that led to a miracle taking place," she said nervously, her eyes on the verge of tears, "then I feel like He wanted us to fall in love . . . and get married . . . on Christmas!"

Wally looked nearly overwhelmed with happiness. "Then let's do it! Let's get married today!"

"Thank you!" she whispered to him.

He kissed her hand again and looked up at her. "Can you see if the hospital has a chaplain and if we can have a wedding today?" he asked.

She patted his arm softly and then stood up. "I'll get right on it!"

Aleta rushed down the hallway to the floor's main nurse station. Two woman and a man were there. The closest nurse, a slender middle-aged woman with short red hair, briskly walked up to meet her.

"Is something wrong, miss?" the nurse asked, alarmed.

Aleta shook her head. "No. It's just, um, Wally and I want to get married, here in the hospital, today. Is that possible?"

"Is there some rush? Your fiancé is going to recover," the nurse replied. "He might even be released tomorrow."

The other female nurse, who was larger and had shoulder-length blonde hair, joined them.

"Wally—my fiancé and I—we experienced a miracle last night," she began. Over the next couple of minutes, she shared the details of their incredible situation. "So, we both want to get married today, if we can."

Rhonda nodded. "The chaplain isn't here. He's having car problems."

"What about Pastor Howard?" the other nurse suggested.

"Aleta, this is Kelli," Rhonda added.

"I'm friends with his daughter, Dani," Kelli continued. "I could give her a call."

Rhonda turned her head to look at Aleta. "He's Baptist. Does that matter to you?"

Aleta smiled nervously. "I don't know much about denominations. If he can marry us, that'll be fine."

Kelli gave her a thumbs-up and a grin. "Don't worry, miss. I have a good feeling about this. I'll call right now!"

"Thank you, Kelli!"

This young woman, Aleta, had given Rhonda a renewed sense of hope. The poor thing had just escaped a bad relationship, experienced a real-life miracle, and found real love with an old flame. Rhonda understood why Aleta would want to get married, especially after a Christmas miracle. So, Rhonda wanted to help her.

She smiled as Kelli hurried back to the nurse station a minute later, her expression joyous. Aleta brightened in anticipation.

"He'll do it—today!" Kelli cheered. "He can be here this afternoon!"

Aleta opened her arms and let Kelli give her a sisterly hug.

"You're awesome, Kelli! Wally's gonna be so happy!"

"This is amazing! This will be our first Christmas wedding!" Kelli exclaimed, releasing Aleta.

Rhonda stepped forward. "Aleta, I know this is your and Wally's wedding, but can I let the local news station know about this? I have a friend in the newsroom, and I can give him a quick call."

Aleta looked at her clothes and frowned. Then she considered her bruised face and tousled hair, not to mention all that Wally had been through. "I don't think we'll look too good in pictures or on camera, but thanks anyway."

Rhonda nodded. "I understand. Can I just pass on the information? I can ask my friend not to send any reporters or camera people."

Aleta still felt wary. "Are you sure?"

"I'll make sure of it myself, okay?" Rhonda assured her.

Kelli waved. "I need to check on my patients now. I'll check back in a bit."

"Thanks so much!"

Rhonda was already on her break. She went to the breakroom, grabbed her phone, and made a call.

"Hey, Ed, this is Rhonda," she said. "Have I got a news story for you!"

Ninety minutes later, Aleta stood next to Wally's hospital bed, once more holding his hand. They both faced Pastor Benjamin Howard, a tall, sixty-something man in a black and white suit with a red and green tie. His short, dark brown hair was going white. He looked at the couple through rectangular glasses and smiled.

"We've gone through the paperwork, and I'm convinced you two are of sound mind and genuinely want this," Pastor Howard said with a deep drawl. "I'm delighted to marry you two today on the day we celebrate our Lord's birth. I'd like to begin with a prayer."

He closed his eyes, and both Wally and Aleta did the same.

"Heavenly Father, we praise You today and invite You to this place in the name of Your beloved Son, Jesus Christ," Pastor Howard continued. "Lord, this young man and young woman wish to be joined in holy matrimony. We ask for Your blessing upon their union and their life together. Lord, You were gracious enough to bless them by sparing their lives. Now, please bless them with a beautiful marriage. We thank You and praise You in the name of Your magnificent Son, Jesus Christ. Amen."

Both Wally and Aleta repeated "amen."

"Wallace James Carson, do you take this woman, Aleta Victoria Jiménez, to be your lawfully wedded wife?" Pastor Howard began, moving his gaze from Wally to Aleta and back. "Do you promise to love and cherish her, forsaking all others, so long as you both shall live?"

Wally lifted his head and made direct eye contact with the preacher.

"Yes, I will!" he said, full of conviction.

Aleta squeezed his hand and smiled at him before returning her gaze to Pastor Howard.

"And, Aleta Victoria Jiménez, do you take this man, Wallace James Carson, to be your lawfully wedded husband?" the preacher said, nodding toward Wally. "Do you promise to love and cherish him, forsaking all others, so long as you both shall live?"

She nervously tightened her grip on Wally's hand and straightened her posture.

"Yes," she said proudly. "I will!" She took in a deep breath. As she released it, she relaxed her grip on Wally's hand.

Pastor Howard smiled broadly as he looked at both of them.

"Then by the power vested in me, and in the sight of Almighty God and these witnesses, it is my pleasure to declare you husband and wife. You may kiss the bride!"

Aleta leaned over Wally's bedside and enjoyed their first romantic kiss. It only lasted a few seconds, but it felt so right. When the kiss was over, Aleta lost herself in Wally's gaze. And he couldn't take his eyes off of her.

"We did it, 'Leta!" he exclaimed.

She nodded, barely containing her joy. "Yes, we did!"

Aleta had turned on the television in Wally's hospital room just before nine o'clock that evening. She sat in a chair beside his bed, holding his hand as they watched the local news.

"Did the nurse say when the story was going to air?" Wally asked. Aleta could hear the strain in his voice. He was tired and starting to drift off.

She rubbed his forearm reassuringly. "You can get some sleep if you want. I can tell you about it later."

He looked at her and smiled. "Maybe I should."

Just then, the news cut to a young Hispanic male reporter standing in front of what was clearly the hospital entrance.

"A special wedding happened today," the reporter began with a smile. "Here at the River Valley General Hospital, a couple who nearly didn't live through Christmas Eve decided to get married on Christmas Day. Wally Carson was in a car accident, and Aleta Jiménez helped him out of his damaged truck. But the two were alone in an area of town that had shut down already." The reporter turned his head toward the hospital. "The two braved sub-freezing temperatures and snowfall for hours before ending up at the hospital, where they were treated."

Then he turned back toward the camera. "But there is much more to their story. As it turns out, Carson and Jiménez knew each other in high school and got reacquainted, even while struggling to survive. And once they were out of danger, the two wanted to get married right away. A local pastor, Benjamin Howard from First Baptist Church, was asked to perform the ceremony. He agreed; and this afternoon, they were married."

The camera switched back to the newsroom. "That's remarkable, Carlos!" a young, dark-haired anchorwoman asked. "How are the couple doing, medically?"

The camera returned to Carlos. After a moment, he nodded in response to the question. "Mrs. Carson has been released from the hospital, but her husband will be here until at least tomorrow. The Carsons asked not to be shown on camera or have their pictures shown. They also asked not to have any visitors to allow Mr. Carson to properly recover."

"Best wishes to them," Emma replied, being shown in the newsroom. "When we come back, Bob is going to tell us if we're in for more snow."

Aleta picked up the bedside remote control and turned off the television as it went to a commercial. She peered at her husband, who was already sleeping.

Well, it's official, Wally, she thought. *The public now knows we're married! The reporting wasn't completely accurate about what happened; but at least, it got the point across.*

Chapter 4

The Next Day

"Wally, it's incredible!" Aleta said breathily as she near-glided into his hospital room. "You're not gonna believe this!"

Wally was having difficulty putting on his jacket as he prepared to leave, clearly still weak and hurting some. "What's going on?"

Aleta helped him put on his jacket; then she grabbed his hand and gently pulled him toward the door. "C'mon!"

Once they reached the hospital lobby, Aleta slowed to a stop; and Wally's eyes widened in surprise.

Next to the hospital's Christmas tree display, at least two dozen freshly wrapped presents of varying shapes and sizes adorned the dark green carpet. As Wally moved closer, he saw each of them were addressed to him, Aleta, or both of them. There was also a bag on the floor containing dozens of cards, some enclosed in envelopes, and handwritten notes.

"Where did all of this come from?" Wally wondered aloud.

"The hospital staff said people started dropping them off last night," Aleta replied. "It's like we got another Christmas!"

"We saw your story on the news," a man said. Wally recognized the deep tenor voice of his employer and confirmed it with his eyes.

"Mr. Ryker? What are you doing here?"

Ryker walked closer, his demeanor pleasant.

"This must be the new Mrs. Carson," Ryker said, extending his hand to Aleta. "Congratulations!" She shook his hand briefly.

"Yes, I am," she said, smiling nervously. "Thank you, sir."

Wally turned his head to address her. "Aleta, this is my boss, Thomas Ryker of Ryker's Groceries."

"It's nice to meet you."

"Likewise," Ryker replied. Then he turned to Wally. "I'm sorry to hear about your truck. I came here to offer you a ride."

"You didn't have to do that, sir," Wally said abashedly.

"I wanted to," Ryker insisted. "Really, it's no trouble. My SUV has room for you two and the gifts."

"Wow!" Aleta interjected. "You have a great boss."

"I like her already," Ryker joked, patting Wally on the shoulder. "She's a perceptive young lady."

Ryker pulled up to the hospital main entrance drop-off area in his red Hyundai Palisades. It looked brand new. He helped Wally and Aleta load the gifts and card bag into the back. A few minutes later, Wally and Aleta sat together in the back seats as the vehicle left the hospital parking lot.

"I'm guessing everything in your truck got messed up?" Ryker asked as he halted for a stop sign.

Wally sighed. "Yeah. The police told me it was another miracle that the fire fizzled out before it reached the gas tank. They think the snow and cold temperatures helped. But the cab and everything in it burned up."

Ryker turned right onto Fourth Street.

"I'm sorry to hear that," Ryker sympathized. "I talked it over with my wife, and we'd like to have you both over for a belated Christmas dinner today."

"Mr. Ryker, that's so—" Wally started to say.

"Thomas," Ryker interjected, still looking ahead at the road. "We've worked together for over a year now. You can call me Thomas, okay?"

"Okay . . . Thomas."

"Look, Wally, when I heard how bad things got for you last night, it made me understand that you're not just a good employee and a friend. I consider you family."

Wally was momentarily stunned. "I–I'm honored, sir!"

Hours later, Ryker brought Wally and Aleta to Wally's apartment and helped them take everything into Wally's first-floor apartment. It was already dark, and a bright half-moon shone overhead in the starry sky. They waved goodbye to Ryker from the parking lot as he drove away, then walked hand in hand back to the apartment,

There was a moderate cold wind blowing as he unlocked the door to his apartment. And then, a musty smell assaulted them as they entered. Aleta coughed.

"Sorry," Wally said sheepishly. "I haven't aired it out in a while."

"Do you mind if we do that now?" she asked, trying to sound pleasant.

"No, I don't mind," he said, still embarrassed.

As Wally turned on an overhead light from a wall switch and went to open windows, Aleta explored the living room. The walls were off-white and seemed sparce and bare. Only a medium-sized window with a bland view of the parking lot broke the monotony. Looking down, she saw a faded brown carpet floor supporting a small tan couch against one wall. A twenty-seven-inch flatscreen television faced the couch, mounted on a black table. There was a basic torchiere-style floor lamp at the corner next to the couch. Beyond that, the kitchen area had a typical, unremarkable setup.

She walked past the micro-bathroom and proceeded to the lone bedroom, which was a mess. The bed hadn't been made. And based on its musky odor, she wondered how long it had been since her husband had changed the linen. On the floor, she saw an overflowing laundry hamper and a dozen sports magazines laying at random locations and angles. She wasn't surprised to find empty soda cans on top of the two-shelf wooden bookcase.

It looks like he stopped caring about this place weeks ago, she considered.

Mentally, she couldn't help but compare living conditions. She recalled the house she had lived in with Roman for the past year. It had been big enough for two. She had done her best to keep it clean and make it nice for them with her cute decorative touches. She had run away from that home just like she had run away from Roman.

She was lashed by another flash of memory when Roman hit her in the car. And then, so many times Roman had hit her. She reached up to her swollen face, still sore to the touch. Then she literally shook her head briefly to ward off the unpleasantness.

She startled as she felt Wally's hand gently cover her shoulder from behind. "Are you all right?"

Turning to face him, she felt embarrassed. "Just some bad memories."

He nodded slowly and sympathetically. Then he took her hands in his. She was captivated by the pureness of his gaze toward her.

"I know I don't have much to offer right now, but I can promise you this: I will share all I have with you; I will love you; and I will never raise a hand to harm you."

Those words and the sincerity in his eyes were like a warm light burrowing into the cold darkness she had endured for so long. Her heart clasped onto it and felt such relief.

He's still so honest, she thought.

"I believe you," she replied reassuringly. "And hey, I don't have much to offer, either. I don't have a job, but I can get one. And I can help around here until we can get a bigger place."

Wally turned his head to visually inspect the apartment. "You're right. The size of this place was okay when it was just me. I didn't need much." Then he looked at his wife and smiled. "But it's not just me anymore."

She shook her head and gave him a slight smile. "Nope."

Just then, she could finally feel a breeze wafting through the apartment.

"You only have a single bed," she noted with some disapproval.

"Errrr, yeah. But the couch folds out to a full-size bed," he countered, pointing toward the living room.

"That'll do for tonight," she acknowledged. And then she found her sense of humor. "I wouldn't want you to have to sleep on the floor."

He chuckled. "Me, either!"

He sat down on his bed. "So, um, what about your clothes and stuff?"

She sat down beside him and looked toward his open closet. "Right. My stuff. I guess I'll have to rent a moving van and go over to the duplex." She sighed. "I really don't want to deal with Roman . . . but I need my clothes. And there's a few keepsakes I want, too."

"You know I'm coming with you, right?"

She smiled at that. "Thanks. But we can do that tomorrow, okay?"

He nodded, still looking at her. "All right. What do you wanna do now?"

"Are you kidding? Let's go open our presents!"

The next morning, Wally woke to the sound of Aleta humming. He didn't recognize the tune; but her sweet, lilting tones made him smile, even before he opened his eyes. She was lying next to him, still wearing her purple sweater, gazing at him with curiosity and intrigue. He was still sore all over, especially his head. *But I'm alive,* he thought. Aleta's swollen and bruised left eye looked painful, too. *We're both hurt and damaged,* he reminded himself. *But we were given a second chance.*

"Good morning," he said, looking up at her.

"Good morning," she replied with a smile. "How are you feeling?"

"I've been better."

She nodded. "I know what you mean."

"We'll both need time to recover, but I feel good about us. I love you."

She nodded in agreement. "I love you, too."

And they kissed.

THE OPPOSITE OF LUCK

ERIC LANDFRIED

A FIST THE SIZE OF a Christmas ham slams into my gut, buckling my knees and bringing the meager contents of my stomach flooding from my mouth in an acidic spray. The two men standing over me—a Samoan mountain and a short, beady-eyed Latino—jump back with groans of disgust as my vomit spatters the blacktop.

"Man, whatchu hit him so hard for?" asks Marco, the Latino.

Hemi, the Samoan, shrugs. "You said hit 'im, so I hit 'im. Not my fault he can't take a punch."

I don't look up at them, resting on all-fours as I spit, trying and failing to clear the bitter taste of bile from my mouth. My bare hands, spread palms down on an uneven sheet of ice, ache from the cold. Marco steps closer, his gleaming, polished wingtips sliding into my line of sight. Despite all my pain and discomfort, I think about how that's the wrong kind of shoe to be wearing on a wintry day.

"You need to pay what you owe," he says, "I ain't runnin' a charity here."

I spit again before I speak. "I will, Marco. I promise. I just need more time."

"I ain't got no more time to give, *amigo*. You been freeloadin' way too long." He looks to Hemi. "Search 'im. Let's see what he's got."

Hemi grabs me by my jacket and flips me over, sending me sprawling onto my back. With one dinner plate-sized hand pressing on my chest, he rummages through my pockets with the other. And of course, he finds the hundred bucks stashed inside my jacket—my last hundred, the one I had Auntie Ellen hold because I knew I'd try to bet it otherwise.

"He got a hundred," says Hemi, handing the cash to Marco.

"Hundred ain't much of five grand," says Marco as he recounts, "but it's a start."

"C'mon, Marco, that's money for my kid's present!" I cry out. "It's Christmas Eve! Have a heart!"

Marco slips the money into his pocket, then steps close and squats next to me. Hemi looms over both of us, eclipsing the gray sky.

"All you betting fools are the same," Marco says, his voice sliding into a mocking tone. "Don't take my money! I gotta eat! I gotta pay my mortgage! I gotta buy my kid a present!" His voice slides back to its normal tone. "And you're all liars. You probably don't even got a kid, man. And if you really do, I feel sorry for that kid."

He stands up, and he and Hemi both take a step back. "I want my money, Teddy. Tomorrow's a holiday, so I'll be with family; but after that, I'm gonna be houndin' you every day until you pay up. And no more bets until you clear your debt!"

He spits on the ground next to me, then spins on his wingtips and walks away. Hemi looks at me—sadness and maybe even a little compassion in his eyes—and says, "He's serious, Teddy. Find the money, or I'm gonna have to do stuff I don't wanna do."

He follows after Marco, then turns back for a split second. "Merry Christmas, Teddy."

I give a frustrated wave, and they both exit the alley, disappearing around the corner. I let my head fall back against the blacktop, and the cold seeps into my skull. A few stray snowflakes drift across my line of vision, but I barely see them, focusing my mind's eye on all the choices that brought me to this moment—all the choices that alienated my family, destroyed my marriage, and now have left me lying in a filthy alley next to puddle of puke on Christmas Eve. And the worst feeling is the emptiness of my pockets, which somehow drops an unfathomable weight on me. I can't buy Caleb's present, can't see the joy in his face when he opens it to see the very thing he wanted more than anything. I promised Leah, my ex, I would get the present, even made sure to leave the money with Auntie Ellen so I wouldn't be tempted to bet it. But now it's gone, and all I have is yet another reason for Leah to hate me and for Caleb to be disappointed. I feel a sob coming on and try to hold it back, but it forces its way from my chest.

Look away, please. There's nothing more pathetic than a grown man, desperate and disheveled, weeping in a dirty alley.

Caleb isn't like other kids. I don't mean that he's disabled or weird, or anything like that. He just thinks on a different level than most kids. He's pretty brilliant, sees things that kids don't normally see. I think he's an old soul, waiting for his nine-year-old body to catch up.

Most kids these days want the hottest new gadgets, but Caleb couldn't have any less interest in that stuff. He has zero interest in video games, smartphones, social media—all that junk. He has a tablet but rarely uses it, except to search for information online. He loves science and literature; and this year, he gave my ex a very short Christmas list. He wants a telescope—a really nice one that costs a couple hundred bucks. My ex is getting it for him. She has a better-paying job than me, and she also doesn't blow her paycheck on sports betting. The only other item he asked for was a set of leather-bound hardback books—a collection of classic literature by Twain, Dickens, Kipling, Wells, Burroughs, Poe, and a few others. There are a dozen or so titles in the set. It runs for ninety-five dollars at a local bookshop, and my ex says Caleb literally bounced on his feet with excitement when he spotted it in the shop window. She asked me if I could get it for him, and I promised her I would. I promised I'd set the money aside.

Oh, man, I'm in such trouble now.

THE GARISH, COLORED CHRISTMAS LIGHTS outside Auntie Ellen's building flash nonstop, giving me a headache. I lean on the buzzer for her apartment until I hear her voice crackling through the intercom.

"What is it? Who's there?"

"Hey, Auntie, it's Teddy. Can you let me in, please?"

"Teddy? Is everything all right?"

"Yeah . . . well, no, not really. Can you please just buzz me in?"

I yank the door open at the sound of the buzzer and enter the building. That old, familiar smell—a weird blend of BENGAY and beef stew—wafts under my nose. I hope when I get up there in age, I don't end up in one these old folks' tenements; but then, I realize that I'd be lucky to land in a place like this, considering how broke I am.

The elevator takes too long, so I hit the stairwell, climbing two steps at a time. By the time I emerge into the fourth-floor hallway, I'm out of breath. As I'm walking down the hall, an apartment door opens; and a scowling, little old woman glares at me as she puts a finger to her lips and shushes me. She then slams the door way louder than anything I was doing. Two doors down, another door opens; and Auntie Ellen peers out, dressed in her nightgown, her thick glasses magnifying her big brown eyes.

"Hey, Auntie."

"Come on in, Teddy. Merry Christmas."

"Yeah, merry Christmas."

I enter her apartment—a small, cramped space she's filled up with an ungodly amount of clutter. She goes to her chair and shoos Mr. Mervin, her cat, off the cushion. Mervin takes one look at me, drops an indifferent hiss, and disappears into the bedroom.

"Sit down, Teddy. Tell Auntie what's wrong."

I shove a stack of tabloid papers over and take a seat on the sofa. I've been mulling in my head how I'm going to explain this; but I still don't really know how, so I just blurt it out. "I lost the hundred, Auntie— the money for Caleb's present."

"Oh, Teddy, you didn't gamble it, did you?"

"No, I—" I pause, considering how much honesty is required here. I decide she doesn't need the details. "I got mugged, Auntie. Two guys jumped me and stole it."

She stares at me, her magnified eyes blinking before narrowing into a skeptical glare. "I've known you your whole life, Teddy. I know when you're lying to me. Now, tell me the truth. Did you gamble that money away?"

I sigh defensively. "No, Auntie! I swear I did not bet that money!"

"It was that little Mexican fella, wasn't it? He found you and took it."

"He's not Mexican; he was born here. He's just Hispanic." I pause, realizing I had no idea Auntie Ellen knew Marco. "Wait, how do you know about him?"

"Oh, he came by here last month. He was looking for you, said you owed him money. I told him you owed a lot of people money; and he said he was the worst of all of them, so you'd better pay up."

"And you're just now telling me this?"

"Oh, stop with the attitude. What would telling you change? You'd still owe the money, and you'd just have more anxiety on top of that."

"Well, I'll worry about that later. Right now, I need money for Caleb's present."

"So, what were you expecting me to do? Why are you here?"

"Well, I was hoping I could borrow a hundred from you. I can pay you back next week."

"Seriously, Teddy? Look around you. I live in this tiny apartment with a smelly cat. Does it look like I have an extra hundred dollars lying around to throw at your problems? I'm on a fixed income, and I barely live on that."

"I was literally on my way to buy Caleb's present, Auntie. I was gonna be a great dad for once. I can't help that Marco took the money."

Her eyes narrow even more. She's really mad now. "You can't complain when somebody pushes you back into the hole you dug for yourself. You shouldn't have been digging in the first place."

The truth in her words stings me hard, and whatever protests I had ready have disappeared. I know this is all true, and I want to change it. I just wish I knew how.

I stand, brushing cat hair off my pants. "I'm sorry I wasted your time, Auntie. I'll get out of your way."

She also stands. "You're not in my way, Teddy. I love you because you're family and because you're all I have left to remind me of my sister. If I could help you, I would; but you also have to face the facts that your problems are your own making."

I nod, feeling shame creeping over my face. I'm sure it's bright red now. "I love you, too, Auntie. But I don't know how I'm gonna fix this."

"Have you tried talking to Leah?"

"Why would I do that? She'd just scoff at me, use this as yet another reason to prove divorcing me was the best decision she ever made. I don't know if I can take that from her."

"You want to be a good father? Swallow your pride and admit your mistakes. That's the first step to teaching your son how to be a good man."

I take a long pause. She's right, but I don't want to admit it. I use all my will to push my pride out of the way and say, "All right, Auntie. I'll think about calling her."

We walk to her door, and I feel her hand on my arm. When I turn, she plants a moist kiss on my cheek. "Merry Christmas, Teddy. You are loved. Never forget that."

"Merry Christmas, Auntie. I love you, too."

She closes the door behind me; and I stand in the hallway, debating whether or not I should call my ex. Finally, I make a decision and head for the stairs.

THANKS TO ALL MY GAMBLING, my credit is absolute garbage. So bad, in fact, that I can't even get approved for a regular cell phone and have to settle for the pay-as-you-go kind. When I take it out to call Leah, I realize I only have six minutes left. Knowing how she'll react to me asking to borrow money, I'm not sure that's enough time. I call her, anyway. She must recognize my number because she sounds annoyed when she answers.

"Hello?"

"Hey, Leah."

"Where are you? You get the books yet?"

"Actually, I kinda ran into a problem."

She sighs. "You bet the money didn't you?"

"No, no! It's not like that. I had the money. I was on my way to the shop, and then—"

"And then what?"

"Marco found me."

She falls silent on her end, so silent that I wonder if my minutes have run out. I take a quick look at my display and see four minutes remaining.

"You're gonna break his heart again," she finally says.

"I know, and I don't want that. That's why I'm wondering if I can borrow the hundred from you and pay you back next week."

"You don't even have a hundred in the bank?"

I know my face is flushing with embarrassment as I say, "I have twenty-seven dollars in the bank."

She sighs again. "Well, I don't have it either. I paid for that telescope with a credit card, and I know it's gonna come back to bite me next month."

"What about Brad? Could he help?"

"I am *not* asking my boyfriend to pay my bills for me, and I'm certainly not gonna ask him to loan money to my deadbeat ex-husband. Besides, he's not exactly swimming in cash, either."

I hear a bustling in the background, and my son's faint voice says, "Is that Dad? Can I say hi?"

"Talk to your son," Leah says to me. "I got stuff to do."

A second later, Caleb's cheerful voice rings in my ear. "Hey, Dad! Merry Christmas!"

"Merry Christmas, buddy."

"Are you coming over soon? I'm so glad we can be together for Christmas!"

"I'll be there as soon as I can. Got a few things to take care of first."

"Okay, Dad, we'll see you soon! I love—"

Caleb's voice is instantly replaced by a cheerful automaton. "We're sorry, but your phone has run out of minutes. To order more, call—"

I end the call. I don't need some robot trying to sell me stuff I can't afford. My heart sits heavy with sadness and frustration as I slip the phone back into my pocket.

What am I going to do?

THE DIM FLUORESCENT SIGN ABOVE the barred windows of Artie's Pawn flickers as I approach, almost as if it's warning me not to bother. I hate dealing with a scumbag like Artie, but he's all I have left. I'm all out of chances here.

The bell on the door rings as I enter the dingy shop, passing through shelves of dusty junk to the counter in the back. The stuff out on the shelves is worthless, and Artie know that; so he leaves it out for potential shoplifters. They're actually doing him a favor when they grab any of it. The valuable stuff is in the back room behind the counter, where Artie sits behind a sheet of bulletproof glass. He's staring at me with a pompous grin as I walk up.

"Why am I not surprised I'd see you on Christmas Eve, Teddy?"

"Hey, Artie, wondering how much you can give me for this phone."

I pull the cell phone from my pocket as he opens up a panel at the bottom of the glass. I slide the phone through, and he snatches it up, examining it closely.

"This ain't even the current model, Teddy. It ain't worth much."

"But how much?"

"Since it's Christmas, I'll show a little mercy. Twenty bucks."

"C'mon, Artie, that phone was ninety brand new."

"Yeah, but brand new was two years ago. Electronics always depreciate. Plus, I gotta make my money back, ya know? I'm runnin' a business here, not a charity."

"You sound like Marco."

"You start comparin' me to that weaselly, little dirtbag, I'm gonna drop my offer to ten."

"No, I'm sorry, Artie. I didn't mean it like that. I'll take what I can get."

"Okay, twenty for the phone. What else you got?"

I search my whole self, finding nothing else of value, except maybe the cheap digital watch around my wrist. I slip it off and slide it toward the glass.

"How about this?"

Artie takes the watch and looks it over skeptically. "I hate to tell ya, kid, but I've seen fast food toys with more value than this thing. It ain't even got a brand name on it. I buy it from you, it ends up out there on the shelves; and you're just gonna blow that money with Marco."

"No, it's not like that, Artie. I'm tryin' to scrape enough together for my kid's Christmas present. I really need you to help me with this."

Artie frowns, pursing his lips together. "You know, I'm not one to fall for the tuggin'-on-the-heartstrings bit, but maybe the holiday season is makin' me feel a little more generous."

"So what can I get?"

"Ten bucks—my Christmas gift to you."

"Fine. I'll take it."

His ancient cash register gives a cheerful ring as the drawer pops open and he takes out thirty dollars. He opens the panel and slides the money through. As my hand closes around the cash, his hand grabs mine and squeezes painfully, forcing me to look him in the eye. There's the old scumbag I know.

"This is a favor, you understand?" he says. "You're gonna owe me one now."

"I thought you said it was a gift."

"It's whatever I say it is because it's *my* money. You come see me after the holidays, and we'll square up. I have a couple errands you can help with."

I nod quickly, and he pulls his hand back, slamming the panel closed. I stumble my way out of the shop, shoving the thirty bucks in my pocket, planning to never set foot in Artie's Pawn again. Of course, knowing myself, I wonder just how long I'll be able to stick to that plan.

So I have thirty now, and I can hit an ATM to add twenty from my account. I'm halfway there, but I'm also out of options. I know this feeling of desperation—know it very well—but this time, it feels even worse because it's my kid I'm letting down, not some scummy loan shark.

With a heavy sigh, I head to the convenience store up the street. I know there's an ATM there.

I look up at the colorful storefront sign for The Bookworm, where a smiling cartoon worm wears a mortarboard with the tassel hanging over his left side. Customers swarm many of the other shops on the street, but only a handful of people peruse the racks inside the bookstore. I guess nobody reads anymore.

I stare at the set of books still sitting in the window, imagining Caleb opening them, seeing the delight in his face. I want that. I've been absent and unreliable in his life, and I'm tired of it. I want my son to look at me and see an example of the kind of man he should aspire to be. But when I think about being that man, it feels so far off—like longing for a trip to Jupiter.

My hand slips into my jacket pocket and feels the fifty dollars crumpled in there. I look past the window display to the woman behind the cash register. She's older—maybe in her late fifties—with curly silver hair framing her face. Black glasses with pointed ends give her a sort of academic look, and the friendly smile she gives a customer makes me think that maybe I could reason with her. Maybe fifty bucks could be enough.

I cross the street, noting a beat cop standing on the corner, watching people enter and exit the stores. He glances at me, but his eyes quickly move on to others. I appreciate his vigilance, especially for a guy being forced to work on Christmas Eve.

The woman looks up as I enter the store and flashes that warm smile as I approach the counter.

"Hello, how may I help you?"

"Uh, yeah, I'm, uh, interested in that set of books in your window."

"The classic set? Of course."

She retrieves the set from the window, setting it on the counter in front of me.

"It's so nice to meet someone else who appreciates the classics."

"Actually, it's for my son."

"Oh? How old is he?"

"He's—he's nine."

Somehow, her smile grows even warmer. "Well, I'm so glad to hear that. It gives me hope for future generations. Now, with tax, that set will be ninety-nine dollars and forty-two cents."

With my hands shaking in a nervous tremble, I pull the crumpled money from my pocket and place it on the counter. "So, uh, here's the deal. I only have fifty right now; and I'm really hoping I could leave it with you, take the books, and then come back next week with the rest."

She instinctively rests a protective hand on top of the set. "Sir, I'm sorry, but I don't know you. If I engaged in those sorts of unorthodox business practices, I . . . well, I wouldn't be in business anymore. I *must* have the full payment."

"This is all I could scrape together," I tell her, despair rising in my voice. "I can't let him down. I just can't."

"Well, isn't there someone to borrow money from?"

My words come out in a snarl. "Lady, if I had someone, I wouldn't be here pleading my case to you."

Her smile disappears. "Well, there's no reason to snap at me, sir. I'm not responsible for your lack of money."

"No, but you'll be responsible for my kid's disappointment if you don't let me take these books."

Anything left of her cheerful disposition fades away, replaced with indignation. "I will *not* be responsible for *your* poor life choices, sir. If your son is disappointed tomorrow morning, then take a long look in the mirror and stop trying to blame complete strangers for your problems."

I'm angry now, my pride wounded. I glare at this woman, the only obstacle between me and Caleb's love. My rage simmers inside me as my hands grip the edge of the counter. She stares me down, matching my glare.

"Sir, I think it's time you left my store. There's nothing for you here."

I will *not* let Caleb down. My hand grabs a basket of designer bookmarks from the side of the register, and I fling it into her face. Stunned, she steps back, and I use the split second to grab the set of books. I tuck them under my arm and bolt for the door. Just as I push it open, she cries out, "Stop! Thief!"

With a victorious smile, I dash up the street, once again picturing Caleb's joy over the books. I'm so caught up in my daydream, I don't even see the arm that snakes out, catching me across the throat. My feet swing up and out from under me, the set of books flying from my hands. My back hits the sidewalk hard, knocking all the wind out of me. I feel myself being shoved over onto my stomach; and as handcuffs click around my wrists, my cheek pressing into cold concrete, I realize I've completely forgotten about the cop standing on the corner. As he reads me my rights, I look over to the book set, lying sideways in a snowbank. It's less than two feet away from me, yet it couldn't possibly be further out of my reach.

The police station bustles with a number of uniformed officers and a motley assortment of people who've been arrested tonight. The two cops who picked me up after the beat cop arrested me shove me forward, heading for the booking area. The noise level in the room maintains a loud but tolerable volume; so when a giant, drug-crazed, biker-looking dude goes nuts and starts roaring and punching cops, everyone's head turns.

"Cuff him to that bench, and let's go help," one cop says to the other.

The second cop frees one of my wrists and pushes me toward a wooden bench, where an old man is sitting. I sit down, and the cop attaches the open ring of the cuffs to the arm of the bench. He then joins his partner. The old man looks at me and smiles though split, bleeding lips. One of his eyes is surrounded by an ugly purple bruise, but it twinkles all the same. He stares so long that I start to feel uncomfortable, so I try to make conversation.

"Did the cops do that?" I ask, gesturing to his face.

"Oh, no. It wasn't the police. They've been very helpful tonight. I was mugged earlier, and they brought me here so I could give my statement. I'm just waiting for my daughter to pick me up."

"Sorry you got mugged. Sounds like you're having the same kind of Christmas Eve I'm having."

"Well, I haven't been arrested, so yours is probably a little worse than mine. What did they pick you up for?"

I feel my face warming with shame, but there's something about this old man that makes me comfortable enough to admit what I did. "Shoplifting. I tried to steal a set of books my son wants for Christmas."

"Oh? You couldn't afford them?"

"I was able to at first. I saved the money and was on my way to buy them, but my bookie and his muscle caught up to me. The day's been downhill ever since."

"Hmmm. So you're a gambler with no money, which tells me you're not a very good gambler. Why don't you stop?"

I pause at his words. Leah has been asking me to stop betting for years, but I just keep doing it. Same with Auntie Ellen. I consider all the relationships my betting has strained, alienated, or even destroyed; and I realize that no matter how much I regret those consequences, I still don't stop betting. I look at the old man, past his injuries, really seeing him for the first time. His eyes radiate kindness, his smile warm and inviting. Usually, when someone starts criticizing my life choices, there's a certain animosity behind it; but I don't sense that here. His kindness opens my mind and eyes to a possibility I've always denied until now.

"I guess . . . I guess I don't stop because I can't. I think . . . I think I might be an addict."

The old man nods solemnly. "What is it about the gambling that draws you to it?"

"Well, it's gotta be the rush when you win, especially when you win big. It just puts you on top of the world. Problem is, once you've tasted that high, you go looking for it over and over. And before you know it, your bank account is empty; and your marriage is over."

"You're chasing joy in a system rigged against you."

"Yeah, I suppose you're right. But chance plays a part in things doesn't it? I mean, nobody loses *all* the time. Well, except me, apparently. Lots of people have luck, despite the odds. But me? I guess I have the opposite of luck."

"No, you don't."

The confidence in his voice stuns me. Did that black eye affect his vision? "Look, old man, I'm a born loser. I got that taste of winning once years ago, and I've been losing ever since. Luck is something I don't have much experience with."

"You and I are viewing luck from two different perspectives. You think the opposite of luck is misfortune because you think everything happens by chance. I know that luck doesn't actually exist because I trust in the Lord, Who writes all our stories and rules over them. There is no luck, no chance, no coincidence. There is only God. He is the true Opposite of luck."

Oh, great. They've handcuffed me next to some religious nut. Just when I thought the day couldn't get any worse.

"So, what are you saying, old man? That God decided I should have the worst Christmas Eve of my life? That I should have to disappoint my son, even though I finally did things right this time?"

The old man nods. "Yes, and He also decided I would be beaten and mugged, all so you and I would end up on this bench together."

"That's gotta be one of the craziest things I've ever heard," I say, wondering how much longer those cops are gonna leave me sitting here.

"Have you read much of the Bible, son?"

"Do I *seem* like a guy who's read the Bible?"

He ignores my sarcasm and keeps talking. "There's a book called Lamentations that contains a pretty profound and astonishing statement. It says in chapter three, verses thirty-seven and thirty-eight, 'Who has spoken and it came to pass, unless the Lord commanded it? Is it not from the mouth of the Most High that good and bad come?' God brings both good and bad into our lives for our own good and for His glory. Everything that has happened to you and me today has brought us to this moment because the Lord wants you to hear the Gospel from me."

"So this is where you tell me all about Jesus dying on the cross? I'm not sure I'm interested in that, old man. I just want to get my son those books and make him happy. But it's all out of reach now. What I could really use at this point is a Christmas miracle."

"The greatest miracle has already happened, but you're too caught up in your own problems to see it."

"Oh yeah? And what miracle is that?"

"Picture it: the eternal Son of God leaving behind all the riches and glory of Heaven, casting aside every right and privilege, and condescending to mankind—to sinners, to those who stand in rebellion against him. He is a King, yet His first rest is not in an extravagant cradle but in a feeding trough for animals. He isn't wrapped in a soft, comfortable blanket but in rags used to wipe sweat off those same animals. He isn't born indoors, where it's safe and warm, but out in the open, among the animals. The first proclamation of His birth isn't made to a royal court but to a bunch of blue-collar shepherds stuck working the night shift. He lives his entire life with little more than the clothes on His back, and even those are stripped off and gambled away as He goes to die the worst possible death—a criminal's death. Jesus made Himself as low as possible, so that sinners like me and you could be lifted up. The amount of love, mercy, and grace it takes to make that happen—that's the *real* miracle."

His words have a strange effect on me. I'm not ready to convert or anything, but my defenses have come down a bit. I no longer think he's a nut.

"So how does Jesus dying lift me up?" I ask.

"He becomes your Substitute. He stands in your place and takes *your* sin onto Himself. He takes the punishment you deserve and offers His own righteousness in return. If you want that righteousness, repent of your sin. Give up this idol of the gambler's high. Worship Christ instead. You will find unending joy only in Him."

"Dad!" cries a woman's voice.

We both look up to see a middle-aged woman approaching the bench. The old man's eyes brighten even more, and his smile grows wider. "Hello, honey."

The woman looks at her father and scowls. "They could've at least cleaned you up a bit."

"Oh, I'm fine. It looks much worse than it feels. I'm just glad I can still take a punch at my age."

He tosses a mischievous smile over to me with that last sentence, and I can't help but smile in return.

"Come on, Dad; let's get you home. Everyone is waiting and worried," says the woman.

The old man stands. "This is my daughter, Kathleen, by the way. And what was your name?"

"I'm Teddy."

"Nice chatting with you, Teddy. I'm Philip. My friends call me Phil."

"Am I your friend?" I ask, feeling a small amount of insecurity.

"Everyone is my friend until they prove otherwise. Think on the things we talked about, Teddy. And know I'll be praying for you."

As he turns, the woman gives me a polite smile, and the two of them leave the station.

Now he's gone; but his words remain, bouncing around inside my head.

THE TWO COPS WHO BROUGHT me in forget about me, and I end up cuffed to that bench for half an hour before one of them remembers. They rush me through the booking process; and after two quick mugshots, I'm sitting in the drunk tank, wiping ink-stained fingertips on my pant leg. A handful of guys occupy the cell with me, two of them passed out on the floor, snoring loudly.

Another guy sits on a bench, slouched against the wall, slurring over and over, "I gotta get home. I gotta see my baby girl."

All the others sit quietly around the cell.

The mumbling drunk starts to get on my nerves, but his words sink in, and I realize I'm not very far from where he is. I might be sober, but my situation is just as hopeless as his. I stand and walk to the cell's bars and call out to the officer sitting at the desk by the door.

"Hey, how soon do you think before I can get out of here?" I ask.

He rolls his eyes at me. "It's Christmas Eve, buddy. You need to go before a judge, and there ain't no judges workin' tonight. Best you can hope for is day after Christmas; and even then, it might not happen that quickly."

My heart sinks in my chest, leaving a sick feeling in my stomach. I'm going to let Caleb down, and I'm powerless to change that. I shudder as I consider how Leah will hold it over me, declare me unreliable and untrustworthy. She might even go so far as to never let me see him just to "protect" him from me. Depression creeps at the edges of my mind, and I want to fight it off; but I'm not sure I have the will.

Another officer enters the cellblock and calls out, "Teddy Brooks?"

I look up at the sound of my name, curious and bewildered. "Yeah, that's me."

He comes to the cell and unlocks the door. "You're out. Lady you stole from isn't pressing charges. You're free to go."

Stunned, I rise slowly from my seat. "Are you serious?"

"Nah, I love pranking prisoners on Christmas Eve," the officer says sarcastically. "Way more fun than going home to be with my family. Get out of here. Your dad's waiting to take you home."

"My dad?"

My father died ten years ago, when his body shut down from all the booze he poured into it. He literally drank himself to death. So who's here to pick me up?

As I emerge from the cellblock into the squad room, I get my answer. Phil stands waiting, his hands in his pockets, a wide smile beaming from his face.

"Hello, Teddy."

"You did this? How? Why?"

"I just wanted to see if I could help you, so I did. I talked to the lady at the shop, explained your situation, convinced her to drop the charges. But she wants an apology, so we're going over there now."

There's a little voice in me that wants to resist apologizing, to avoid admitting my wrongs. That voice is an idiot. I'm not spending Christmas in jail and missing my son.

"Okay," I say, a smile of relief spreading across my face. "Let's go."

THE CROWDS ON THE STREETS have dwindled, most of the shoppers finishing and heading home to family. The woman behind the counter looks up as Phil and I walk through the door; and a reserved, perfunctory smile appears.

"Hello, Phil," she says. "And your name is Teddy?"

"Yes, ma'am."

"Teddy has something to tell you, Sheila."

Sheila crosses her arms and looks at me. I step forward, my tongue in knots, uncertain at first what to say; but then it just pours out of me.

"I could stand here all day long and make excuses for what I did. But no matter what my circumstances were, I wronged you. I stole from you. And I'm really sorry I did that to you."

Sheila softens at my words, unfolding her arms. "I forgive you, Teddy. And I was so sorry to hear the turn your life has taken. I would listen to Phil if I were you. He seems like a very wise man."

"And now," says Phil, "how about that package I ordered, Sheila?"

With a pleased grin, Sheila lifts a gift-wrapped box from behind the counter. I realize it's the same shape as the book set and turn to look at Phil.

"I—I can't afford that. I don't have enough."

"Well, I do. So I can buy it; you give it to your son, and you can pay me back when you're able. And I promise I won't beat on you when I come looking for my money."

"But how do you know I won't just gamble the money away when I get it? You might not ever see that money again."

"We're friends now, Teddy. I'm here for you, and I'm going to help you."

Emotion floods my face, threatening to manifest itself in tears; but the macho idiot in me holds them back. "Thank you, Phil."

"Merry Christmas to both of you," Sheila says as she hands me the present.

Phil tips an imaginary hat. "Merry Christmas, Sheila. And remember my invitation. My church's doors are always open."

Sheila smiles and nods as we leave the shop.

Outside, the world seems lighter, brighter even. It feels like that same high I've gotten the handful of times I actually won from betting. I never knew you could feel this high without risking your money.

But as we walk to Phil's car, the last voice in the world I want to hear calls out to me.

"Yo! Where do you think you're goin'?"

Phil and I both turn and see Marco and Hemi approaching us. My high disappears as quickly as it came. Here's the evidence that I'm a born loser, destined to be that until the day I die. Teddy Brooks isn't allowed to have a happy ending. God has decreed it.

Marco and Hemi herd us into a nearby alley, and Marco points to the present in my arms.

"So you got money to buy gifts, but no money to give to me? I don't think so."

"I loaned him that money," Phil interjects. "I bought the present."

Marco sneers as he looks Phil up and down. He shows a mild curiosity at Phil's black eye but stays focused and says, "Don't know who you are, old man, but any money this *perdedor* gets comes straight to me. He don't get to borrow money for presents as long as he owes me. Now you gonna pay his debt, old man? You got five G's in your pocket for ol' Marco?"

"Of course not. Why would I walk around with that much money on me?"

"Okay, then. You ain't got the money, then you give up that present."

"No, Marco," I say, clutching the present tighter against my chest. "You can't take this. It's for my kid. I gotta get it to him."

Marco spits a hawker on the blacktop, then crosses his arms. "Okay, here's the deal. Either you give up the present, or I have Hemi pound you into pulp; and then I take the present, anyway. Make your choice."

Phil pushes me back against the wall and stands in front of me. He looks at both of them. "If you're gonna beat someone, beat me. Then Teddy can get home to his family."

Marco scowls. "Hemi, this old man is really startin' to get on my nerves. Put him down."

I look at Hemi and see disbelief in his eyes that Marco would demand he beat up an old man like Phil. The pause lasts long enough that Marco looks up at him in angry surprise.

"Did you hear me, you big dummy? Put this old man down!"

Hemi shakes his head. "Nah. I ain't beatin' up an old man. It'd be like punchin' my grandma. You want it done? Do it yourself."

Rage flares in Marco's eyes, and he shakes his finger at Hemi. "You and me are gonna have a long talk later about doin' what I tell you."

He then turns to Phil, his hands clenched tightly into reddening fists. "You sure you wanna take Teddy's beating, old man?"

"Show me what you got, son," Phil says, raising his fists.

"I ain't your son, and you ain't *mi padre*," Marco says, just before launching a right jab.

I flinch as I expect the punch to land; but Phil surprises me, dodging it and retaliating with a right cross to Marco's jaw. Marco staggers back in disbelief, rubbing his jaw, then attacks again, this time with more fury. Phil fends off the first few punches, but his age catches up to him; and after a few blows to the head, he crumples to the ground.

But Marco doesn't stop. He plants a kick into Phil's side, and the old man groans in pain. I want it to stop, but I know about the straight razor in Marco's pocket; so I don't dare try to intervene. Marco squats, waling on Phil with his fists; and I'm scared Phil's going to die when Hemi reaches out and catches one of Marco's fists in mid-air.

"That's enough," he says, his baritone voice carrying an authority I've never heard before.

Marco spins, his face a mask of ugly wrath. "Let go of me! *I* say when he's had enough! Not you!"

"You're an ugly man, Marco," Hemi says. "I ain't gonna work for somebody who does this."

"You can't quit me!" Marco screams. "I'll cut you! I'll cut your family!"

Hemi's normally placid face twists into an angry scowl at the threat; and with his other hand, he grabs Marco's torso, lifting him into the air.

"Hey!" Marco cries, his rage instantly transforming into panic. "What are you doing?"

Hemi turns and plants a screaming Marco headfirst into an open dumpster. The impact must have knocked him out because his scream cuts off and his loose legs flop over into the trash. I help a bruised and battered Phil to his feet.

"Why did you do that?" I ask Phil. "Why take my punishment? I mean, I deserve what Marco's dishing out, not you."

"I just did it, Teddy," says Phil. "I didn't want you all bruised and bloodied when you meet your son. But as I think about it, I guess it's also an object lesson."

I catch his meaning. "You're talking about Jesus being my Substitute, like you just were."

Phil nods. "Yes, but Jesus did it on a much greater scale than I ever could."

"You should take the old man to the ER, Teddy," Hemi says. "Get 'im checked out."

I look up at this giant man, someone I once feared; and now, I see only his humanity. "Thank you, Hemi. But what will you do when he comes after you?"

Hemi shrugs. "He won't. He knows better. That's his dirty little secret. He's the bark; I'm the bite. Without somebody like me, he's nothin'. It'll be a little while before you need to worry about him again."

"Well, thanks all the same."

"Merry Christmas, Teddy. Now pray for me 'cause I gotta go home and tell my wife I'm unemployed." He gives a small grin. "If you think I'm scary, you should meet her."

He lumbers off, disappearing around the corner. Phil and I exit the alley and head for his car.

"You think the ER is a good idea?" I ask him.

"Yeah, I think so," Phil answers. "That kick really hurt. Should get these ribs checked out."

I toss the present onto the backseat and help him into the car. Then we're off to the hospital.

THE HOSPITAL WAITING ROOM WRITHES with people having a far worse Christmas Eve than Phil or I. Sick, wounded, and annoyed people; crying kids; and overworked nurses all crowd together, the patients waiting impatiently on cheap vinyl chairs. The nurses run and spin in a random, dizzying dance, their sneakers squeaking against the over-waxed floor.

After a brief and frustrating argument with the nurse at the check-in desk, I lower Phil into one of the last empty seats, and he lets out a soft groan.

"Thank you, Teddy," he says. "You don't have to stay. My daughter should be here soon."

"Now what kind of man would I be if I just left you here by yourself?"

He looks up at me and flashes a grin. "I appreciate the sentiment, Teddy, but I'll be fine. I'm perfectly capable of handling a hospital on my own." He looks around the crowded room. "Besides, unless blood starts pouring out of my ears, I'm probably gonna be here a while. And you don't want to miss Christmas with Caleb."

He's right, but I still feel guilty leaving him behind. There's also the fact that I don't have any transportation, so I try using that as my excuse.

"Well, you're my ride, so I guess I'm stuck here, too."

Phil shakes his head. "Nope. That's not happening. I'm not going to be the reason a man misses Christmas with his son. You have my keys; take my car. You can return it in a few days. My address is on the registration."

The level of sacrifice this man is willing to endure for me astonishes me. He barely knows me, yet he's given up so much.

"Come on, I can't just leave you here. It's my fault you're here to begin with!"

Phil frowns and shakes his head. "No, it is *not*. Marco attacked me, not you. You've got enough of your own sin to bear. Don't add his to the pile."

"But this happened because you helped me."

"And that was God's intention for our good and His glory. And while he brought me this pain, He also brought relief when He moved Hemi to stuff Marco into that dumpster."

A small smile spreads across my lips, and I remember the look of shock on Marco's face.

Phil sees it and smiles as well. "Don't get me laughing, or it'll hurt more," he chides with a warm grin.

"I still can't believe you took those punches for me when I've never done anything for you."

"And I say the same thing every day about Jesus. He took my punishment when all I had to offer Him was unholy rebellion. As

Jonathan Edwards once said, 'You contribute nothing to your salvation except the sin that made it necessary.'

"Now, it's time for you to go. You don't want to miss Caleb. Take my car and get over there."

"Are you sure about this, Phil?"

He smiles. "The Gospel is the only thing I'm more sure of. Now go."

We shake hands as I fight back my emotions. "Merry Christmas, Phil. And thank you."

"Merry Christmas, Teddy. And you're welcome. Now go."

I turn and exit the room, leaving the clamoring noise of the waiting room behind me. As the automatic doors to the exit slide open, I meet Phil's daughter walking into the hospital. She stops, looking me up and down.

"He's okay," I say. "Just a little banged up."

She sighs before leveling her gaze at me. "I really hope you're worth all this."

I try to meet her eyes with my own, but find I can't. I stare at the ground instead, feeling my face flushing red with shame.

"Me, too," I say.

A second later, she's gone; and I leave the hospital.

THE FIRST THING I NOTICE as I pull into the driveway are the colorful lights Leah has strung along the gutters of the house. They're the same kind of lights as the ones outside Auntie Ellen's apartment building; but this time, they don't annoy me or give me a headache. Has something changed in me? I'm not entirely sure.

With the present under my arm, I jog up the steps and ring the doorbell. A few seconds later, the door opens; and Brad stands before me. Good, old Brad: pudgy, reliable, and safe. It's no wonder Leah went for a guy like him after the six-and-a-half years of fear and anxiety I handed her.

"Hey, Teddy, we weren't sure we'd be seeing you."

"Hey, Brad. I wasn't so sure myself. But I made it."

"Well, come on in. Caleb's going to be psyched you're here."

I enter and set the present on the floor, shrugging out of my jacket. Leah walks in from the kitchen, a glass of wine in her hand. She spots the present on the floor, and her lips spread into a surprised smile.

"You got it," she said. "After you called, I thought for sure you wouldn't get it."

I return her smile. "I had a little help," I say, pausing for a second. "Actually, it was a *lot* of help."

"Well, regardless, I'm so happy to see we can finally have a nice Christmas together."

Brad takes my shoulder in a friendly grip. "How about a beer, Teddy?"

"You know, Brad, normally I'd say sure, but I think I want to keep a clear head tonight."

Brad shrugs. "Sure, man. Whatever you want. I'm going to go check on dinner."

He slips past Leah into the kitchen. She takes a sip of wine, her eyes examining me.

"You look different," she says.

"I do?"

"Yeah, you don't look so . . . beaten down. I don't think I've seen this side of you since we were first married. Did something happen today?"

I shrug. "I finally started winning—but not from gambling. Things have suddenly started going in my favor."

"Well, let's hope this lucky streak keeps going."

"I'm beginning to think luck has nothing to do with it."

"Dad!"

Caleb, tall for his age and lanky, appears from the living room and makes a beeline for me, grabbing my waist in a crushing bear hug. I stoop down and wrap my own arms around him.

"Hey, buddy, it's so good to see you."

"I'm so glad you're here, Dad."

He looks past me to the present; and being the smart kid he is, he recognizes the shape.

"You got me the books! Oh, thank you, Dad!"

I didn't think his hug could get any tighter, but it does; and all the emotion I've been suppressing all day comes pouring out of me. Fat tears roll down my face, and a hoarse sob escapes my throat. Caleb pulls back from his hug and looks at me, deep concern behind his eyes.

"Dad? What's wrong? Why are you crying?"

It takes a moment for the words to come, but they do. "Oh, buddy," I sob, "your dad is *so* broken!"

An awkward silence fills the room. Neither Leah nor Caleb know how to respond to my declaration. Finally, Caleb says, "Well, if you're broken, can you be fixed?"

I look at him and smile through my tears. "That's the good news, buddy. Today, I met Someone Who *can* fix me. An old man introduced me to Him, and I think He's already changing me."

Caleb looks a little confused, so I just pull him in close again, hugging him tightly.

"Merry Christmas, buddy," I whisper in his ear.

"Merry Christmas, Dad," he mumbles into my shoulder.

Leah cradles her glass of wine, staring at me intently, a wondering smile dancing on her lips.

A TICK IN TIME

PARKER J. COLE

Part 1: An Absolutely Beautiful Day

Aiea, Hawaii
December 7, 1941

"What a beautiful day," Elizabeth Lucas remarked as she stood on the passenger side of her husband's newly purchased fiery red Ford Super Deluxe. It was ten in the morning, and the day was as peaceful as any other. Soon, her favorite holiday, Christmas, would be here.

Just as her husband reached forward to open the door, Elizabeth placed a hand on his shoulder. "Zeke, after service, why don't we take a drive?"

Zechariah bent and gave her a kiss on the cheek. "You don't think I brought this beauty to simply admire it, do you?"

She laughed as he waggled his bushy eyebrows. "Very well."

"After twelve years of marriage, you should know me by now."

Elizabeth cupped the left side of his beloved bearded face. "There's always something new to learn about you," she said softly.

His eyes gleamed as he kissed her palm. "That's my girl."

Pulling apart, Zechariah opened the door for her; and Elizabeth got in, tucking in her dress. As Zechariah closed the door and went around the front of the car, she looked out of the window. Clear skies filled the horizon providing a spectacular view. In the distance lay the Ko'olau Range, a steep mountain range with sharp peaks and well-defined ridgelines of long-ago volcanic activity. Shrouded in mist, the sight of it created a serene backdrop.

A feeling of well-being filled Elizabeth as she gazed around. Their modest, single-story, wooden house had a sloping roof and was surrounded by a small yard, a couple of mango trees, and a tiny vegetable garden she enjoyed working in. With the holiday nearing, she missed the snowy days of her youth while in New York; but she still got into the Christmas spirit, dressing up their humble domain with boughs of artificial holly and a few strings of lights and setting out the Nativity scene in the front yard. They lived in relative privacy, close enough to get help from a neighbor if needed but still isolated enough to maintain their own need for seclusion.

When she married Zechariah twelve years ago, Elizabeth had no idea she'd be content on this island away from the mainland. But satisfied she was, and she thanked the Lord for that.

Zechariah opened the door and got in, dispersing her inner musing. "Did you hear that thunder?" he asked.

Elizabeth frowned. "Whatever are you talking about?"

"I thought I heard thunder just now."

Leaning forward, she peered out through the windshield. "It doesn't look as if it's about to storm." She glanced at Zechariah. "Are you sure you heard it?"

He pursed his lips and said nothing for a few seconds. "Perhaps I imagined it," he said finally. "Look at that view. How could there be—"

Something smashed onto the windshield.

Elizabeth screamed as her arms went up, shielding her from the shattering glass. The next instant, Zechariah yanked her into his arms and tucked her head into his chest, using his body to protect her.

After a long, heart-stopping moment, Zechariah moved off her. "Be careful, my love," he urged. "Are you hurt?"

Elizabeth gulped. "I'm fine, Zeke. What about you?"

He pulled back. Except for his wide, dark eyes and the thudding pulse at his neck, he looked none the worse for wear. "I'm fine. I was more worried about you."

"What was it that fell onto the—oh my!"

Elizabeth stared in shock at the sight of a fully clothed, short-haired man lying across the broken windshield.

"What on earth—!" Zechariah nearly kicked open the door as he got out the car. Elizabeth followed suit. Together, they stood at the front of the car, staring at the prone figure.

"I don't understand what's happened."

"I don't either." Zechariah glanced up at the sky. "Surely, he didn't fall from up there?"

Her husband pushed her behind him in a protective stance as the man moaned and then turned around.

"Ridiculous portals," the man mumbled.

Elizabeth's head cocked to the side. Strange noises crackled from a small metallic strip attached to the man's neck at the same time unfamiliar words came out of his mouth.

How odd.

Still groaning, the man moved gingerly off the car. He was of average height with toasted-brown skin. As he started to brush off his clothes, Elizabeth gaped. There wasn't a scratch on him. Before she could question it, the man was speaking again.

"What day is it?" the man asked.

Zechariah exclaimed, "What day is it?" He flailed his arms around. "You've crashed into my new car, nearly killing my wife, and you're worried about today's date?"

"Please," the man urged. "What day is today?"

"It's December 7," Elizabeth answered, lifting onto her tiptoes to peer over Zechariah's shoulders.

The man stilled, and his light-colored eyes bulged. "It can't be!"

He whirled around in a sort of mad circle, gazing at the sky. "It can't be!"

Zechariah snorted. "What can't be?"

The man fell to his knees, his pained face lifted toward the sky. "It's a clear sky, partly cloudy." His voice choked with tears, he shouted, "It's an absolutely beautiful day!"

Elizabeth blinked. "I've never heard of anyone complaining about a beautiful day."

"He doesn't have anything to be upset about," Zechariah grumbled. "It's not his car damaged by a lunatic that fell out of the sky."

The man jerked back to his feet. "Neither of you understand. The last thing this day is supposed to be is a beautiful day. There should be military personnel here, radio messages, and news reports being announced everywhere."

"Are you referring to the naval base?"

The man scowled. "Of course, I am!" He dragged his fingers through his thick hair. "Nothing has happened?"

Zechariah threw his arms in the air. "You destroyed my car!"

The man looked over his shoulder at the vehicle. "This is more concerning than your vehicle," he said with some frustration. Then he looked at the sky again. "How could it be such a beautiful day?"

"Sir, you're not making any sense," Zechariah grumbled.

"I know." The man let out a long breath.

"No, you're not making sense at all." Coming out from behind Zechariah, Elizabeth took a step forward. She pointed like a five-year-old. "What is that strange metal thing on your neck?"

A strange stillness overcame the man. "You can see that?"

"Yes."

Zechariah looked at her with concern. "What are you talking about? There's nothing unusual on his neck. He's just unusual in general. Are you sure you're all right, Liz?"

The man's eyes narrowed on Elizabeth in a rather suspicious way. He then tapped once on the metallic strip on his neck. "I don't have much time," he said.

Elizabeth noticed that the crackling noise ceased. "Why not?"

"We have to figure out why this is such a beautiful day."

"That may have something to do with the weather," Elizabeth replied blandly.

"Sir, who *are* you?" Zechariah's voice filled with incredulity.

"I'm Adus Hytenoch." He thrust his hand forward. "Won't you shake my hand?"

"Why?" Zechariah's left eyebrow arched. "Are you trying to trick us or some such thing? We shake your hand, and then we won't report you for damaging my car?"

"Isn't this how your people greet one another?" he asked.

Slowly, Elizabeth said, "We usually say we're pleased to meet you."

"Oh. I must have embedded the wrong custom from the database . . . Well, no need to worry about that. In fact, why shake hands at all? I'm here to make sure your country goes to war."

PART 2: ADUS HYTENOCH, THE TICK

"GO TO WAR?" ZECHARIAH'S BROWS lifted far into his forehead. "What on earth are you talking about?"

A cold hand had gripped Elizabeth's heart. She couldn't have said anything, even if she wanted to. She was too stunned by what this peculiar man had said. Her eyes remained fixed on Adus' bronze-colored face as he spoke.

"At this moment, this island should be in the middle of a military lockdown." Adus flared his nostrils. "There should be pandemonium."

"But why do you say we're supposed to be at war?"

Adus eyed her. "Why do you think? If your country doesn't go to war, then the future will be changed."

Zechariah grabbed Elizabeth and pulled her back. "Stay away from him, Liz; he's one of those wackos."

"No, I'm not!" Adus exclaimed. "I know what I'm saying is hard for you to believe, but we have to instigate a war."

As incredible as it sounded, Elizabeth had the feeling that this Adus Hytenoch was telling the truth. There was something mysterious going on.

"Why should we believe you?" she asked. "More importantly, why should we have anything to do with 'instigating a war'?"

Adus was silent for a moment. Elizabeth sensed that he was trying to determine *what* to tell her. Then he sighed. "Because I'm a T.T.C.— Time Travel Coordinator. A 'Tick,' for short . . . in your vernacular."

A breath lodged in Elizabeth's throat. *He's a time traveler!*

Zechariah scoffed. "You've obviously had thousands of ticks in your brain, eating away at the gray matter. 'Time travel'? That's nonsense!"

Elizabeth put a steadying hand on Zechariah. She understood her husband's skepticism, but something urged her on. "Wait, Zeke. I believe he's telling the truth."

A look of relief washed over Adus. "Thank you."

"Why? He's not making any sense at all. And he destroyed my new car."

"How else would you explain what's happened here, my darling?" Elizabeth reasoned in a soothing voice. Zechariah was a gentle man most days, but Adus Hytenoch did destroy his new car. He was allowed to be a bit peevish.

A part of her wondered if she might have lost her mind; but the more she thought about it, the incredible became the probable. What other explanation was there? Was this the gift she'd prayed for all these years?

"But even if what you are saying is true, I don't understand how you think we can instigate a war. Zechariah's an associate deacon and teacher. I take care of our home. And even if it was possible, why would we want to? War is terrible." Elizabeth's thoughts drew inward, seeing her father's writhing form entangled in sheets on a narrow bed, bathed in sweat, features wreathed in agony and that terror-filled blind gaze.

"But it is a necessary evil at times," Adus replied, tugging her out of her memories. "If this war does not happen as it's supposed to, then the future will be irrevocably changed."

Elizabeth gently freed herself out of Zechariah's grasp, but she held onto his hand. "What do you mean, you are a T.T.C.—or 'tick'—as you say? What is that?"

"The Tick counters the Tock."

"Tick, tock!" Zechariah exclaimed in disbelief. "Are you trying to make fools out of us?"

"Shh, Zeke. Let him finish."

Adus glared at her husband, but he kept going on. "The Ticks have a peaceful purpose. In what you would call the distant future, our technology allows us to observe all of time: past, present, and even future. When it becomes necessary, some of us have the means to travel forward or backward in time. We try to avoid it, though. The risk of tampering with past or future history is great, as you will see."

"So, you're from the future?" Elizabeth shook her head in confusion. "Why have you come to our time? And what does that have to do with this war you're speaking of?"

"The Ticks honor the preservation of past and future history and the integrity of time, but the Tocks do not," Adus replied. "They are T.T.C.s from a different point in the future. They believe in selectively altering history to correct what they see as 'missed opportunities' or 'mistakes.' It is a flawed philosophy and tends to be self-serving. The Ticks have to remain vigilant in our observations of time and be ready to restore the timeline when the Tocks interfere," Adus said, though his voice trailed off. "Look, I know this is a lot to take in."

Elizabeth's eyes roved over him, and she drew in a sharp breath as she read his eyes and somber expression. Her mouth gaped open; and hurriedly, she tapped Zechariah on the shoulder. "Zeke! He's telling the truth."

"What do you mean, Liz? You believe this madman?"

Adus had turned his attention back to her, his eyes narrow.

"He's not a madman," she said breathlessly. "He's a human being like us, and I sense that he's telling the truth."

Adus sighed. "I am telling the truth, but I'm not entirely human like you," he added. "What enables me to travel through time are small machines that have been surgically embedded within my body. We try to shield it from view; but some people—like you, Mrs. Lucas—can perceive us as we truly are."

"The metal strip on your neck," she stated.

Adus nodded. "That is one of the machines, yes. I can't explain what they all do, but they are important."

"We can't help you unless you tell us what is going on," she insisted. Elizabeth couldn't suppress the burning curiosity that swept through her. Only a few short minutes ago, all she'd been concerned with was going to church and then a drive.

"Liz, we should be contacting the police, not entertaining wild fantasies from some man who damaged our car," Zechariah suggested.

"What if he's right, Zeke?" she countered. "What if history has been changed somehow, and we could help set it right? Don't we have an obligation to help?"

Zechariah took a calming breath before addressing his wife. "Perhaps, my love . . . but even if he is somehow right, we can't start some kind of terrible war."

"Fine. I'll just show you," Adus said. He waved his hand, and a sudden sound like thunder—but far louder and stronger—boomed through the air all around them. The sky darkened. Swollen, gray clouds and streaks of lightning like thin, minute scars across someone's face marred a once-clear day.

Zechariah wrapped his arms around her as she asked, "What's happening?"

"That's the same thunder I heard before," her husband said.

"It's not really thunder, just camouflage for our exits and entries. For now, take my hand. I want you both to come with me to the future."

Part 3: Hope in Time

"You're not really considering this, are you?"

Elizabeth gazed at Zechariah, her teeth digging into the flesh of her bottom lip. "We have to, Zeke. Surely you can see that."

"He could be trying to take advantage of us." Zechariah stabbed his finger in Adus's direction. "He may be making up these things."

Yes, Elizabeth considered, *but what if he's offering hope instead?*

She'd read H.G. Wells' *The Time Machine* many times, always fascinated by the story. After what had happened to her father in the war, she'd had this childlike wish to do what the time traveler had done—go back into history. Unlike the time traveler, though, she wouldn't want to change the history of the earth. What could she, a nobody in the grand scheme of things, ever provide the world at large? Elizabeth had no special talent, just a painful past that only affected her. But if she could change history for her father, didn't she owe it to herself to try? An intense longing rose within her. Was this an answer to her prayers?

She had to find out if the past could be changed.

For you, Father.

"Consider what we already know, Zeke. He knows things, and he literally fell into our lives. Aren't you a little intrigued?"

Zechariah said nothing as he stared at her. She waited, holding his gaze without saying a word. The incredulity vanished from his face in slow degrees as he lifted his finger to caress her cheek.

"It's what you've always wanted, isn't it? To break through time itself and make a difference? The Christmas gift only the Almighty could give you?" Tears stung her eyes, and she nodded with undeclared hope. Zechariah understood why she needed to do this. He knew why she had to discover whether what sounded like insanity might indeed provide clarity for her. "All right, Liz. We'll do this." Once again, Zechariah grabbed her hand into his. "Lord, protect me and my wife as we do this very odd thing. Thy will be done. Amen." He kissed her forehead and then drew back.

"Excellent!" Adus stuck out his hands. "Both of you, grab on."

Apprehension filled every part of Elizabeth's being, but underneath it simmered a latent excitement. Was she really going to go to the future? Would she really be able to help her father?

She grabbed Adus' right hand, while Zechariah grabbed his left. In that instant, an electric charge stung her hand and then grew in intensity, piercing every part of her body with burning pain. She tried to pull away, to cry out even, but was unable to. In fact, she went blind, consumed by darkness and light at the same time. The pain increased until in her thoughts, she begged to die.

Suddenly, the pain stopped, and she collapsed. Onto what, she didn't know. It didn't matter. All she knew was the sweet liberation from pain.

"I'm sorry that hurt so much. It will pass," Adus said. "The only advantage our implants give us is that they protect us from the pain of time transition."

"Do be quiet, you Tick," Elizabeth heard Zechariah grumble. "Where and when are we?"

She recognized that they were inside a building with metallic walls and some kind of machinery woven into those walls. She wasn't familiar with the exact type of metal. It didn't look like steel, brass, or even aluminum. There were windows on the walls to her left and right. And some kind of cityscape was visible through the windows.

"I'd rather not say the year, but we are in what you would know as North America," Adus replied.

"It's called something else now?" Elizabeth asked. "Whenever 'now' is?"

"Yes," Adus confirmed. "You can take a look at the metropolis outside. That will confirm we are not still in your time."

"We'll see about that . . ." Zechariah began to say when he went suddenly quiet. He was closer to one of the windows than Elizabeth, so she joined him at his side and marveled.

It was nighttime outside, but she could see buildings of various shapes and heights with lights on inside or on top of the buildings. They stretched on for miles in every direction. There were strange, floating lights in different parts of this city.

Then she saw something zoom by. It was small and looked like a mixture of automobile and airplane, sleek and dark blue with small lights in the front and back. Its shape reminded her of a dart. *Is that a flying car?* she wondered. *Nothing like that exists where we came from!*

"This isn't a window; it's some kind of projector playing a film!" Zechariah declared in disbelief. "You're still trying to trick us, sir!"

Adus calmly walked over to the window and pressed a button next to it. The blinds slid back, and the window submerged into the wall.

Clean night air wafted in, and the scene outside remained the same. "I assure you, sir, this is real."

Zechariah gaped in amazement. "S-so it is!" He coughed. "Maybe you'd better start at the beginning."

"Fair enough," Adus replied. He motioned them to a table and chair in the corner of the room. Once they were seated, Adus continued. "The people like me, the Ticks, we have a responsibility to observe all of time. And sometimes, we see a disturbance that registers in our equipment. These disturbances are almost always caused by another faction that calls themselves the Tocks."

"You mentioned them before," Elizabeth interjected.

"Why do they alter time?" Zechariah wondered aloud. "Doesn't that complicate things?"

Adus nodded. "Indeed, it does. But they want things changed."

"Why?" Zechariah added.

"They believe they have a more enlightened perspective on history," Adus said with some derision. "If they don't like how a historical event unfolded the way they believe it should have, they go back and 'repair' it. They are aware their interference will have a ripple effect on other historical events; but if it falls within what they consider an acceptable range, they make the change, anyway."

"And that's why this war that was supposed to happen isn't happening?" Zechariah asked.

Adus nodded. "Exactly!

Elizabeth spied the expression in Zechariah's eyes. It was too much. "Adus, can you give us a moment of privacy, please?"

"Of course."

Once the Tick had sauntered away, Elizabeth reached across the table and grabbed Zechariah's hand. "Are you upset with me for insisting we come here, Zeke?"

"No, Liz, I could never be upset with you about this." He kissed her fingers. "I know the Lord wouldn't have us here if it wasn't a part of His plan. So, it doesn't matter, really, as long as I'm with you."

How could it be, after twelve years and now in some distant future in a place she never could have imagined, Zechariah's love for her still made her blush as if she were a new bride? Her expression must have conveyed her inner feelings because Zechariah took her hand and rubbed it along the contours of his face as though her touch were a blessing.

Thank you, Lord, she prayed. *I am not alone in this. Even here, the evidence of Your love resides between me and my husband.*

Gathering her thoughts together, she said, "Adus seems to think that a deacon and a housewife can somehow right this wrong to history." It was still incredible to think about. Still, after all that Adus had shown them, how could it not be true? "We need to talk about this and figure it out."

Zechariah continued to toy with the tips of her fingers, but his gaze was skeptical. "By instigating a war? How could that even be possible?"

"Oh, Zeke." She gave a helpless laugh. "Don't be so cynical. Maybe we don't have to actually start the war. But, um, perhaps we could learn what prevented it?"

"All right," he replied, letting go of her hand. "Where do we start?"

"We need to find out when the Tocks changed history."

"They could have tampered with any point in the past, right?" Zechariah said. "How would we know when?"

Her mind reeled from the rather strangeness of it all. But being a learned woman, she tapped into her experiences. "We need a book—a history book." She turned around and spoke to Adus. "Is it possible to give us a history book? One that shows how things are supposed to be?"

"We do have one that was acquired before the timeline changed. It shouldn't be affected. I'll fetch it."

When Adus came back from where he had gone, he carried a large book with him. Placing it on the table, Elizabeth saw it had the title, *History of the United States*. Opening it up, she glanced at the copyright page and saw the year. "Nineteen eighty-one? Forty years from now?"

There was cursive handwriting in the book scrawled on the first page, but she couldn't make out the words as it had been smudged over time. With a shrug, she browsed through the table of contents until she came to the section that said, "The Japanese Attack Pearl Harbor." It had been circled in bright red ink.

"So, it's true," she said. "We were supposed to be attacked."

The idea frightened her. According to the details she read as she browsed the pages, the Japanese indeed attacked on December 7, 1941, at eight o'clock in the morning. Her eyes ate up the words as they recounted the waves of attacks that struck the Hawaiian Islands in two waves. She was shaking by the time she finished reading about the destruction.

"It's awful," she whispered.

Adus sighed. "Now you can see why I was dismayed."

Elizabeth pushed the book away. "But why should we want this? What's wrong with having a world without war?"

"We asked ourselves the same thing." Adus tapped on the table between them. "But each tampering with history, even the preclusion of war, can and does have drastic ripple effects on events following whatever changes are made. It can cause people who were supposed to live to die, prevent people from ever being born, and lead to the fall or rise of entire civilizations."

"How?"

Adus looked uneasy. "There can be secondary effects from a temporal altering—what you might call a law of unintended consequences."

Elizabeth shared a look with Zechariah. He was a teacher, after all. Clearing his throat, he said, "Well, from what we know, Japan doesn't have any dealings with the United States. As a matter of fact, even in the war, we were allied; but there were tensions between the Japanese forces and the United States. We did try to open trade relations several times throughout the years." Zechariah pulled at his beard in thought. "I recall an incident that took place some eighty years ago. A colonel of some standing went to Japan and tried to establish some sort of trade relations, but they weren't successful."

"Why not?" Adus asked.

Zechariah's face went slack. "There were reports that the man had gone mad."

"In what manner?"

Elizabeth saw Zechariah's eyes widen. "In his diary, the leader spoke of strangely dressed creatures who told him to not set foot onto the Japanese shoreline. In fact, when the Japanese saw the 'Black ships'—what they called the United States vessels of the time—they were frightened at first. And then, suddenly, the ships turned away and never came back. Accordingly, the Japanese have seen our country in a rather weak light since then."

"Eighty years ago." Elizabeth looked through the table of contents once more, seeing an entry called "The Perry Expedition to Japan: The Opening of Japan to the Western World." She read it out loud.

"Let me see." Zechariah took the book from her and read through it. "It says here that Matthew Perry was a commodore who used gunboat diplomacy to force Japan to open their borders to trade to the United States."

"He did?"

Zechariah's brows drew inward as he read. "It seems after hundreds of years of self-isolation and limited trade with other countries, this Perry Expedition caused the country to enter the world market; and it expanded their growth as a world power."

"But that would lead to their bombing of us. Wouldn't it be better to avoid that?"

"Liz, wait."

She glanced back at Zechariah and saw his face had paled. "What is it?"

"This history book says that we, the United States, would eventually do something horrific."

"Such as?"

He pushed the book back over to her, placing his finger on the titled section.

Her voice quivered as she read out loud. "'The United States Ends World War II With Bombing of Hiroshima and Nagasaki.'"

The more she read about the destruction her country had caused to thousands of innocent people, the sicker she felt. "I can't believe it." Glaring at Adus, she said, "And you want us to somehow cause this to happen?"

"You have to," Adus insisted.

"We can't!" Elizabeth stood. "Even if by some minuscule chance we had the ability to do this, we won't. We won't be responsible for the deaths of all those people."

"Don't be so arrogant, Elizabeth Lucas."

The tone in Adus' voice stopped her. It was filled with censure. "What do you mean?"

"You might not otherwise have a significant impact on history," he began.

"That's a wordy way of saying we're nobodies, isn't it?" Zechariah mumbled.

"But here and now, you might be able to fix this problem and restore history to the way it was, bringing about the attack that leads the United States to enter this war," Adus continued. "But if this timeline continues, your country will face a far worse attack."

"Speak plainly," Zechariah demanded.

"In the proper timeline, the bombs that eventually ended the war were developed by the United States and its allies, but they weren't the only ones working on them. The Germans worked on those bombs, too. If this timeline is allowed to continue, Germany will develop the bombs first. And over the course of three days, they will drop five bombs – two on the United Kingdom and three on the United States. And that will destroy the Western world as you know it." His eyes were hard as diamonds as he spoke. "Elizabeth will be killed during one of those bombings."

"But you said we're nobodies!" Zechariah cried out.

Dryly, Adus retorted, "Everyone knows the names of the dead."

Elizabeth's knees weakened.

"Do you see what's at stake now, you two?" Adus implored. "We have to find the Tock who altered history!"

Zechariah brought Elizabeth into his arms. Placing frantic kisses along her forehead, he whispered over and over, "I can't lose you, Liz. I can't."

She shivered violently and rested herself against Zechariah's strength. "I don't want to be without you, either. We have to make things right again."

Part 4: The Diary of Commodore Matthew Perry

ELIZABETH WISHED SHE HAD NEVER come here. She wished she were back in her own time, that she and her husband were driving along the scenic routes of the island. She wished she had never met Adus Hytenoch, this Tick in time who was ruining her life. This was the worst beginning to the Christmas season she'd ever experienced. The saying that ignorance was bliss never rang so true as it did for her this moment.

"It has to be the Perry Expedition!" Zechariah exclaimed.

"What?" Elizabeth asked.

"The change had to be from the Perry Expedition," he clarified as he leaned forward eagerly. "Matthew Perry, in the original timeline, forced the Japanese to trade with the U.S. The ramblings of the captain then were dismissed as the utterings of a mad man; but knowing what we know now, it must be the Tocks' interference."

Dejectedly, Elizabeth flopped back against the seat. "What does it matter, Zeke? We're nobodies. There's nothing we can do to stop this."

A knowing look appeared in Zechariah's eyes. "You mustn't let what Adus said bother you."

A harsh, humorless laugh escaped her lips. "It's too late for that."

"No, listen to me, Liz. You're letting what he said affect you. You're thinking of your father, aren't you?"

"I—"

"Your father's abandonment of you and your mother was his fault, not yours. He may have made you feel as if you weren't good enough for him to fight for life. He chose the selfish way out. But I'm not him. I'll fight for you—for us—with every breath in my body."

Her gaze lifted. "Why?"

Zechariah's eyes revealed the depth of his love for her. She'd always known that he cared deeply for her; but right now, seeing just how much moved her.

"You're my world, Liz. You mean everything to me. And if restoring a . . . troubling history is the only way to keep you in my life, then I'll do it."

His words were sweet, perhaps even a bit flowery; but in this moment, they coursed through her, giving a new vitality to her. Maybe she was a nobody in the scheme of things, but she was the world to her husband, just as he was to her. "All right, Zeke. I hear you."

She blew out a breath and tried to focus on the task at hand. "If Matthew Perry's expedition didn't succeed, then I agree that must be where the Tock caused the change."

"But how do we figure into this? Neither of us were born then." Zechariah rubbed his beard. "Let me see the book again."

She handed it over; and together, she and Zechariah browsed through the contents of Perry's Expedition. Her eyes rested on the family tree outlined in the book. "Wait, Zeke," she said. "Look here."

"What is it?"

"Matthew Perry married Jane Slidell, the sister of a U.S. Senator."

"So?"

"Look." She pointed to a list of their children. "They had ten children, and one of their children married a colonel named Robert Smith Rodgers."

He shook his head. "I'm not following you."

"The Rodgers! We met them a week ago. They were a couple on their honeymoon."

Excitedly, she jumped up from the table. "Adus! Adus!"

"What is it?" he replied.

She whirled around to see him standing behind her. "We know what it is. The Tock must be in 1853."

"We're in agreement on the year, Elizabeth. But what month and day?"

"From what I can remember reading, the diary entries chronicled the commodore's mental condition. He was insistent that he'd been warned by demonic-looking creatures to stay away and to not complete his mission. When he returned—in disgrace, mind you—he lost much of his prestige."

"But when? If we can get the precise time according to your measurements, then we'll be able stop the Tock."

"Wouldn't that be fruitless? They've already gone and changed the timeline."

"When the Tock tamper with history, they use a machine to blind our technology," Adus explained. "It's to prevent us from finding them and discovering what would happen as a result of their tampering. We can't find them, but they can't see us, either. We need to know the precise date."

"We met Matthew Perry's descendants—a newlywed couple on their honeymoon. We chatted for a while, and we were invited to a dinner with them at a local restaurant. They talked about Matthew Perry, but we never thought much about it."

"Do they have his diaries?"

Elizabeth nodded. "Yes! Mrs. Rodgers told us the diaries were given to them as a wedding gift."

"I need those diaries," Adus declared. "Perry would have recorded his thoughts and events. We'll be able to pinpoint exactly when the Tock made contact."

"But how? We're not close to them, by any means."

Adus smiled. Elizabeth looked away, hearing him as he said, "I'm a Tick, remember? A Time Travel Coordinator. I'll get you to when we need to go. You simply get access to those diaries."

"You'll need to hold onto my hand; and I'll get us to a secluded place near the restaurant, where you'll meet Perry's descendants," Adus said calmly. "With a, er, special gadget of mine, you two will be able to re-live the experience as yourselves with your present memories and understanding—without damaging the timeline. But you will only have a few hours to do so. Do you understand?"

They both nodded.

He handed them each what looked like a sapphire gemstone. "Just keep this in your jacket and purse."

They did as he instructed.

"Now, this is important. What day did you meet the Rodgers?"

"December 1, 1941," Zechariah replied. "It was a few days ago."

"What time?" Adus followed up.

"Two o'clock local time."

"Were you in the restaurant at that time or walking into the restaurant?'

"I guess we were walking into the restaurant."

"Now, I am going to do something the highest level of our council has allowed me to do. During our time transit, I am going to place you inside of your body at this moment. The gems with you will protect you from the pain this time. All you need to do is find a way to get access to the diaries and discover the date Matthew Perry met the Tock."

"But how will we—"

"Don't worry. I'll be watching. Now, both of you, hold my hand. We're about to go."

"Mr. and Mrs. Lucas, are you all right?"

Elizabeth gasped and blinked. No longer holding Adus' hand, she found herself standing in the doorway of the restaurant next to her equally stunned husband.

David and Glenda Rodgers stared at them as if questioning whether both the Lucases had gone mad.

Attempting something like a graceful recovery, Elizabeth said, "We're fine. I think we both just remembered something."

"Are you sure?"

"Absolutely." She gave a forced smile. Glancing behind her, she saw that Zechariah was just as disoriented, but he recovered. "Ah, yes. We should have done that . . . thing."

"Well, we'll worry about it later," Elizabeth said lamely, and they all proceeded inside the restaurant.

The next half hour or so was a long, drawn-out feeling of *déjà vu*. Elizabeth ordered the same meal and drink, had the same conversation, and laughed at the same jokes. She even felt the same warmth as she observed the Rodgers' evident love for each other, making her think of herself and Zechariah when they first married.

"How did you and Mr. Lucas meet?"

Elizabeth glanced over at Zechariah. He took her hand into his. "We met on a bridge in Upstate New York, overlooking a small river. Liz was standing there, and I thought she was going to do some harm to herself; so I grabbed her and spoke kindly with her, offering to take her for coffee, a meal, or home if she wanted."

"And how did you answer him?" Mrs. Rodgers replied with an eager light in her eyes as she gazed at Elizabeth.

"I turned to him with my fishing rod, still trying to put the worm onto my hook, and said, 'I just wanted to catch some fish.'"

They all laughed at that.

"We hope to have children as soon as possible," Mrs. Rodgers said a moment later. "I'd love to have a Christmas baby. Do you have any children, Mrs. Lucas?"

"No," Elizabeth answered. Zechariah's hand squeezed her own. "We learned I am unable to have children."

Mrs. Rodgers looked sorrowful. "Oh, I'm so sorry."

"It's all right," Zechariah said. "It means I have her all to myself."

They laughed again, and Elizabeth almost wept. Most men might have left her once they learned of her infertility, even in this modern day and age. But she knew Zechariah was truly one in a million.

"It seems large families are part and parcel of our family line," Mr. Rodgers interjected. "Most of our ancestors had a lot of children, even the lunatics."

"What do you mean?" Her heart jumped in her chest. *This is it!* Elizabeth thought.

"My husband's family has an ancestor who had ten children with his wife," Mrs. Rodgers said. "He went mad, though."

"Can you tell us about him?" Elizabeth gently asked.

"Oh, he was a commodore in the navy, fighting all sorts of battles—a man of perseverance and great fortitude."

"And a little mean," Mr. Rodgers added as an aside.

Mrs. Rodgers shrugged. "Well, this ancestor was sent by the president of the United States himself to open trade with the country of Japan. They had tried many times before; the country had adopted an isolationist view of the world. This time, my husband's ancestor was sent to make it happen by any means necessary."

"And what happened?" Even Zechariah was leaning forward.

In a conspiratorial manner, Mrs. Rodgers' voice lowered. "Well, Commodore Perry led the battalion of ships to the Japanese shoreline. One could just imagine how they must have looked—dark ships at full mast, streaming out puffs of black smoke from the chutes, with a formidable artillery at the ready. It must have frightened the Japanese at the time.

"Then, according to one of the men on board, Commodore Perry raced out of his cabin, spittle on either side of his mouth, his hair wild and blue eyes filled with terror. With an almost inhuman strength, he lunged at the helmsman and ordered him to turn around. 'Demons!' he cried out. 'Demons have taken over my mind. They have compelled me that nothing but evil can come from this alliance!'

"Well, you could imagine how his men reacted, but they had to obey him," Mrs. Rodgers shared. "And that was the end of the expedition that never happened. Commodore Perry eventually resigned, but the stink of his failure traveled through a couple of generations."

"Incredible," Elizabeth said, careful to keep her voice appropriately neutral, though impressed. "But how did you know so much about it? That must have happened, oh, eighty or so years ago."

"Eighty-eight years ago, and we know because the family kept Commodore Perry's diaries all this time. In fact, I have them with me. I wanted to read about this man during our honeymoon."

"Would it be terribly gauche of me if I asked to read them as well?" Zechariah lifted his hands in a helpless manner. "I'm a history teacher, and something like this truly interests me."

"Oh, that's perfectly all right. I mean, we can't allow you to take them, of course; but you're more than welcome to come back with us to our hotel. We'll bring them down and read them with you."

"Really? That would be wonderful." Zechariah turned to Elizabeth and chuckled. "Who knew that little nobodies like us would be eating with descendants of great people like these?"

THE HOTEL ROOM WAS DECORATED in furnishings of the Christmas season. Behind them in the hotel drawing room, faint greeting sounds of merry Christmas were being uttered by passersby who was close enough to hear them. In the massive hotel hearth, the fire crackled pleasantly in the background, the gentle light providing a soft ambient glow to their surroundings. If it wasn't for the seriousness of their mission, Elizabeth would have just sat and enjoyed the atmosphere.

Instead, she drew her attention back to the manner at hand. "Look at how he describes the demons, Zeke," Elizabeth exclaimed as she carefully turned the weathered page of the diary of Commodore Matthew Perry. "He said, 'Each night for the past three nights, I have been plagued by the visitations of monsters, ghastly creatures of such hideousness that to behold is to behold the face of Satan himself. One appears to me—dark with a lifeless mechanical eye, arms covered in brass, and a metal claw for a right hand—like a demon pirate if ever I saw one.'"

Mrs. Rodger's shook her head. "Commodore Perry was rather dramatic in his descriptions, wasn't he?"

Elizabeth's mouth twisted. *Apparently, Adus is fairly normal for a Tick. That Tock sounds horrific.*

Zechariah tapped her on her forearm. "Hear this, Liz. 'When the demon pirate smiles, his mouth has teeth all made of silver. He is grotesque and refuses to leave me rest, save I stop this trade alliance with the Japanese people.'"

"That poor man," Elizabeth remarked. "Driven insane by his, er, visions."

Mr. Rodgers made a tutting sound in the back of his throat. "Indeed, but what can we do? It's not as if something worthwhile would have happened had he been successful."

They had gone through several of the diaries; but so far, they were unable to see when the Tock's interference happened. If they didn't get it, then how could they—

"Liz," Zechariah whispered in an enthusiastic tone. "I found it."

Her heart jumped into her throat. "When, Zeke? When?"

His eyes gleamed with triumph. "A week before the commodore and his battalion reached Japan."

Part 5: Black Ships

Above the Pacific Ocean
July 1, 1853

"Where are they?" Elizabeth asked anxiously.

Adus had placed them in an airship that hovered above the waters of the ocean invisible to the naked human eye. For several hours, they had been waiting for any sign of the Tock faction. Still, there was no sign of them. The muscles churned in her belly. There was no way she could keep the tension away. Everything they had work toward in these few hours on one single day had led up to this moment.

For the first time, she felt as if she had a purpose.

"Be patient, Elizabeth," Adus stated laconically. "They will be here."

Zechariah held her close. "This is better than taking the drive around the island, isn't it?"

A small smile lifted the left side of her cheek. "Do you regret that your car was shattered for this moment?"

Her husband pursed his lips. "Yes, I still do."

Shaking her head in amusement, Elizabeth scanned the waters once more. After all she had learned, how could she go back to her old life? Maybe after all was said and done, she would do something different with her life. She would not be content to be a nobody anymore.

"There they are!"

She followed the pointing finger to see an odd distortion appear several feet in front of her. The distortion grew, reminding her of heat waves on a hot summer day. Like heat waves, it rippled in the air. The site of the distortion grew and expanded farther out.

Then thunder sounded all around them as a cylindrical-shaped airship like their own appeared.

"Get ready," Adus said to the other Tickers with him.

Just then, a panel outlined in a blue light appeared, and then the strangest creature that Elizabeth had ever seen stepped forward.

Just as Commodore Perry had stated in his diary, the creature looked grotesque with his protruding eyes and darkened flesh.

"They're wearing a mask," Adus muttered. "I used to have the same one when I was a child."

Adus shouted something Elizabeth didn't catch, but a volley of activity ensued from it. Tickers dashed back and forth to consoles, pressing on lighted panels and buttons. Alarms were going off.

The projector screen flashed on, and the image of the Tock came upon it. They looked a little different from Adus and the other Tickers. When the Tock opened his mouth, he spoke in a strange language. Adus answered in kind. There was a volley of speech going back and forth. Each time, the tones of each speaker gathered strength and rage.

Elizabeth and Zechariah watched as the exchange happened, wondering if they were going to be able to stop the Tocks from changing time. There was nothing more they could do here. Then, suddenly, the Tock disappeared from the screen.

"This isn't good," Adus said darkly. "They're not going to come without a fight."

"Why not?"

"I can't tell you right now, Elizabeth. But you and Zechariah get back in the—"

Without warning, the Tocker who had been talking to Adus appeared before them. The Tickers shouted in shock. Elizabeth gasped, but then she was thrown to the ground when something slammed into the airship.

"Elizabeth!" Zechariah cried.

More Tocks appeared on the ship, and they started to attack the Tickers. Instruments and weapons of odd designs were wielded with force. Beams of light flashed from them. Those weapons that were shorter in range elicited screams from the Tickers. Elizabeth, still disoriented from the fall to the ground, stared around her in horror.

Then, a Tocker looking around with a glazed look in her dark eyes, lunged toward Elizabeth.

"No!" she heard Adus scream.

It was too late. Something invisible wrapped around Elizabeth, and pain like she'd never experienced before scorched every fiber of her being.

"Liz!" Zechariah shouted from somewhere, but she couldn't tell.

She could barely hear the sound as the ripping pain scoured through her body.

"What's happening?'

"She's using a time eraser. She's trying to erase Elizabeth from time."

A million knives slid along her skin. She couldn't bear it.

Then, as quickly as it happened, it stopped.

She collapsed to the floor, weakened and spent, unable to do more than breathe; but even that hurt. Glancing up, she saw that Adus had barreled into the Tock, knocking her to the ground.

"Liz!" Zechariah reached for her.

"No, Zeke!" she heard Adus warn. "If you touch her, she'll get you, too."

The Tocker shoved Adus aside and stood again."I don't care! That's my wife."

She tried to protest, but it was more than she could do. Zechariah gripped her in his arms. "Liz, Liz? Ahhh!"

The scream wrenched from him tore her in two, but she noticed he was taking the brunt of the Tocker's weapon. Blood rushed to his face, and his eyes glazed with excruciating pain.

"Zeke, let me go!"

If anything, Zechariah held her tighter, refusing to let her go.

"No! Please! Please, no!"

His grip was loosening, and his eyes dulled. Elizabeth's heart slammed inside of her chest. Zechariah was dying.

"No! No! No! Zeke, please don't leave me."

Behind her, Adus was shouting; but her mind blocked out everything else, narrowing it only to Zechariah's dark eyes. His hold had grown limp and still, and she felt his hand twitch on her as if using every ounce of remaining strength to protect her.

She couldn't let Zechariah be erased from time.

A fire swelled within her, and she growled. *God, please help me!*

She wrapped her arms around her husband, feeling the fabric of time slice through her body. It hurt—how horribly it hurt—but she gripped him around the middle and tugged him underneath her, shielding his body with hers. Then something ripped.

Or snapped.

Or cracked.

There was a flurry of activity, but Elizabeth ignored it, focusing all her attention on Zechariah.

He lay still on the floor, his eyes closed. "Zeke? Please, Zeke, please."

Dear God, please let nothing happen to my husband. Please! I need him more than I need my past to change. I accept my life as it is for it is the gift You gave me. Please, dear God, don't take my husband from me.

She lowered her head and wept, no longer able to pray but only moaning in desperate supplication.

"Elizabeth."

The Voice called to her, unlike anyone's she had ever heard. And she knew Who it was. It was instant recognition. She turned around, finding herself in a brilliant white place. A figure, brighter than light, stood before her, majestic and humble.

She knew. She absolutely knew Who it was.

"My Lord and my King," she cried out, overwhelmed, dirty, small, and frightened. How could the King be here, above time, and she be in His presence?

"Do not fear, my daughter."

And how could she fear? How could she when He was here?

"Adus and his people need you. I put you here for this place and this moment. Nothing that has happened is outside My will."

The awful notion that she wasn't anybody went away. After all, the Lord of all creation was standing her before, and He knew her name.

How could she be a nobody? It was ridiculous to think that what Adus had said actually mattered.

"Yes, Lord."

"Continue the mission I have for you; and soon, you will be blessed beyond measure."

"LIZ?"

She blinked, and she was back in the airship, sitting beside Zechariah as he groaned her name.

"Liz, are you all right?"

Tears trailed down her cheeks. "Yes, Zeke. I'm fine. Are you?"

"I've been better."

He stirred, and she helped him to sit up. His hands shook, but he caressed her face, as if trying to make sure she was there.

"I'm here."

Adus came toward them. "The Tockers have been apprehended. Look below."

She looked down to see the Black ships of Commodore Perry sailing forth in the ocean.

"Now what?" she asked.

"Now, we take you back, and I'm pretty sure what was supposed to happen will."

Part 6: An Absolutely Horrible Day

"And here, we are able to observe the attack of Pearl Harbor through the eyes of Zechariah and Elizabeth Lucas," Adus stated as he watched, along with the other Tickers the decimation of Pearl Harbor.

As always, whenever he took a group on this temporal tour, something within him choked up.

They had saved the course of human history; and for that, they received . . . nothing.

The council had decided to erase the Lucases' memories of their time with the Tickers and the conflict with the Tockers, along with their actions and sacrifices to restore history. It was a cruel thing, but Adus knew it was for the best.

It was inevitable.

Adus listened as he watched the attack, seeing the pensive expression on Elizabeth's face as she and Zechariah listened to the radio tell them that awful news. He could see her face as she gazed at her husband and hear her words as she said, "What an absolutely horrible day."

Part 7: A Tick in Time

Honolulu, Hawaii
December 25, 1961

Elizabeth bent over in pain, hanging onto the counter as the next contraction wracked through her. "Zeke!"

Zechariah rushed into the room, his face etched with worry and excitement. Seeing Elizabeth in distress, he hurried to her side, gently placing a hand on her back. "I'm here, my love," he signed with his hands. "Do you need to go to the hospital now?"

She glared at him. "Of course, I do. The baby's coming."

Her husband rushed off, and she leaned against the counter, thinking that this was the last thing she had ever expected to happen. Who knew that at fifty years old, she would give birth to a child?

She had a full life as an author, who told delightful children's stories of a world called Tick Tock. It was inhabited by humans with odd machinery that made them unique. Where she got the idea to create the stories, she didn't know. It was a year or so after the bombing of Pearl Harbor, when suddenly, an image came to mind—a rather strange being that was part man and part machine.

Together, she and Zechariah started to create fun stories for youngsters that bloomed out of this Tick Tock world from her imagination. She wrote the stories, while Zechariah illustrated them.

After sharing the stories with his students at school for a few years, they made the plunge to see if a publisher would take them. After many rejections, one publisher did; and the rest was history.

For nearly twenty years, they had lived a blessed life, despite the heartache of the aftermath of war, the rebuilding after the war, the changes in government, and even the societal changes happening in different parts of the world. Through it all, Zechariah and she had been upheld by God and their love for each other.

So, it was with a sense of shock that she discovered after thirty-two years of marriage, she was going to be a mother.

Another stab of pain shot through her. "Zeke!"

He raced back to her, his beard fully gray, along with his hair. Motioning with his hands, he carefully led her outside to the new car, anxious to get her to hospital.

Around the time she had learned she was pregnant, Zechariah had started to have difficulty speaking; and the doctors discovered lumps in his throat. Fortunately, they weren't of a malignant nature; but it required surgery, so he hadn't been able to speak during this time.

Their friends had joked that they could almost be a shoo-in for the biblical couple of Zechariah and Elizabeth, even down to the fact that her husband had lost his voice.

Driving along the highway, contractions rifled through her. Elizabeth found a certain solace in that parallel. Just as Zechariah and Elizabeth had been blessed with a son in their later years, she, too, was experiencing a miracle of her own—a child for Christmas!

She bowed her head and thanked the Lord for blessing her beyond measure. She, who had never thought to have a child . . .

Four hours later, a half hour before midnight, her son was born, screaming in indignation. Looking into his wrinkled, red face, a wave of joy and contentment washed over her. When the nurse gave the child to her, she cradled him against her breast. "Zeke, what do you think we should call him?"

Tear flooded her husband's eyes as he gently rubbed at the child's dark curls. Searching around for a piece of paper, he found one and wrote on it. "His name is John."

"Are you serious, Zeke? Just because we're—"

Zechariah held his fingers to his throat and carefully said, "His name is John."

Elizabeth stared at him and down at her son. "Hello, John, my darling angel. Hello."

Unseen by either of them stood a familiar Tick in time.

THE END

IF YOU ENJOYED *CHRISTMAS MIRACLES*, CHECK OUT THESE BOOKS . . .

JAKE TYSON

Vigilante's Light
Freedom's Fight
Heroes' Might
Phantom's Blade
Speedster's Spark
Crusader's Quest

www.creatingforcreator.wordpress.com

DANIEL PEYTON

Remnant

www.facebook.com/DanielPeytonAuthor

LAUREN SMYTH

Stories of the Night
Made for Mercy
With Love from the Past

www.laurensmythbooks.com

ALLEN STEADHAM

Mindfire
Jordan's World
Jordan's Arrow
Jordan's Deliverance
The Former Things
www.allensteadham.com

ERIC LANDFRIED

Solitary Man
Conflicted Man
www.ericlandfried.com

PARKER J. COLE

www.parkerjcole.com